YOUNG MRS. GREELEY

BOOKS BY

BOOTH TARKINGTON

ALICE ADAMS
BEASLEY'S CHRISTMAS PARTY
BEAUTY AND THE JACOBIN
CHERRY
CLAIRE AMBLER
CONQUEST OF CANAAN
GENTLE JULIA
GROWTH
HARLEQUIN AND COLUMBINE
HIS OWN PEOPLE
IN THE ARENA
LOOKING FORWARD AND OTHERS
MONSIEUR BEAUCAIRE
PENROD
PENROD AND SAM
RAMSEY MILHOLLAND
SEVENTEEN
THE BEAUTIFUL LADY
THE FASCINATING STRANGER AND
OTHER STORIES
THE FLIRT
THE GENTLEMAN FROM INDIANA
THE GUEST OF QUESNAY
THE MAGNIFICENT AMBERSONS
THE MAN FROM HOME
THE MIDLANDER
THE PLUTOCRAT
THE TURMOIL
THE TWO VANREVELS
THE WORLD DOES MOVE
WOMEN
YOUNG MRS. GREELEY

YOUNG MRS. GREELEY

BY

BOOTH TARKINGTON

1929

DOUBLEDAY, DORAN & COMPANY, INC.

GARDEN CITY, N. Y.

T187y

TO

SUSANAH

I

THE Warwicke Armes was almost exactly like the other apartment houses that stood in a row at the suburban end of the new Lincoln Boulevard. All of them were great flat-faced cubes rigidly honeycombed into cells; the cells were all of about the same size, all subdivided in the same manner, all decorated (if the leasing agents' enticement was true authority) in the same "Olde Englysshe Style"; and they were all called by the same name, "kitchenette apartments". We need find no very startling evidence for telepathy, then, in the fact that at one time or another almost every woman living in the Warwicke Armes and its kindred cubes likened those buildings to a row of beehives, and, pleased with herself for the simile, wondered if her husband's intellect could ever be lifted to the true appreciation of a poetic mind. Mrs. Henry Hedge, of number 42 on the fourth floor of the Warwicke Armes, gave her husband many opportunities to display this kind of appreciation, although he was nearing forty and, after twelve years of marriage, she had really given up his intellect.

"It came to me in the night again," she said, one summer morning at breakfast. "It comes to me again and again, Henry."

Her tone was wistful and a little melancholy; so was her expression; but Mr. Hedge, a thin, patient looking man always somewhat preoccupied with his own thoughts, made only a mechanically courteous sound of interest.

"Thasso?" he murmured, and with care placed a fresh slice of bread in the electric toaster upon the white painted metal table at which they sat. "Thasso, Aurelia?"

"I woke up thinking it," she said dreamily. "It was about half way between midnight and dawn, I judged, and you were snoring of course; but it was the idea that woke me up, not the noise you were making. I lay there in the dark, going over it and over it, Henry, and if I hadn't been afraid of disturbing you I'd have got up and written it down."

"Thasso?" her husband murmured again; and she too easily perceived that she failed to win his attention. Naturally he heard what she said and upon challenge he could have repeated it, as she knew by experience; but he was not really listening to her; he was thinking of something else. Moreover, this absent manner of his had long since become habitual with him whenever she talked; but she was never reconciled to it.

She sighed heavily, and her voice became plaintive. "I wonder what it would seem like to live with a man who entered into some companionship of thought with me; I do wonder what just one day of that would seem like!"

Her husband's mild glance, still preoccupied, rose momentarily from his toast to her face. "You mean you were thinking some more about beehives, Aurelia?"

"In the night," she said. "It comes over me oftenest then. I wake up and lie there thinking and thinking about it while you go on snoring and not caring whether I'm alive or dead. I get the feeling like I'm trapped by life—trapped in a row of beehives!"

"'S too bad," he said, speaking into his coffee cup. Then, as he lowered it from his lips, he added, "Bees wouldn't trap anybody though, Aurelia."

"You'll never understand," she informed him. "You never have understood and you never will.

It's so strange! I'm living my life out in a cell in a row of beehives and when I wake up and think of it like I did last night it seems to me I'll just go crazy!"

"It does?" he said, not alarmed. "What's wrong?"

"Beehives!" She sighed more profoundly and shook her head. "All these flats just exactly like this one—all of 'em with exactly the same maroon in the furniture and rugs, the same beds that fold up behind false doors, the same hardwood floors, the same kind of linoleum in the kitchenette, the same records for the phonograph, the same programs every night on the radio——"

"Whoa up!" Mr. Hedge interrupted, showing suddenly a little interest. "They don't have to get the same program if they're willing to take a little pains. I got W P Y tuned out last night with no trouble at all, and after that I got seven stations in different parts of the country, some of 'em hundreds of miles away. I got W A P and Z O R and——"

"Oh, dear!" his wife sighed. "You just don't know!"

"I just don't know what?"

"You don't know what I'm talking about, Henry. You never do, for that matter and I don't know why I still go on expecting that some day you will."

Mrs. Hedge's melancholy increased, she uttered a sigh louder than those preceding it, and returned to poesy. "Just poor driven bees in hives, that's all we are!"

"'Driven'? I don't see how we're 'driven' exactly, Aurelia."

"Don't you?" Mrs. Hedge shook her small brunette head in an expressive way she had. "I wish I could ever find time to write down my thoughts, or else could find somebody to write them down for me as I have them. If some good writer could just take down my thoughts and put them into a book I believe it would make a fortune."

"You mean your thoughts about beehives, Aurelia?" her husband inquired; but his tone was respectful and he had no satiric intention.

"Yes; but that's only a little. I have thoughts I don't believe anyone else ever had since the world began."

"What like?" he asked politely but somewhat mechanically, for she had often said this to him.

Aurelia shook her head again. "You wouldn't understand, Henry. You don't even understand about the beehives. You don't understand how shut in and bound down by life I feel when that thought comes over me. I'm just one driven bee in this terrible row of giant beehives."

Henry had an impulse to question the word "driven" again; he was vaguely conscious that it disturbed her metaphor; but he was wiser in not pressing the point, and said nothing.

"Just driven bees," Aurelia repeated sadly. "Bees, bees, bees, bees!"

She meant the commonly known honey bees, immemorial models of communal industry; and thus her metaphor failed upon another point of accuracy. She should have had in mind the Mason Bee; for to that more selfish insect the resemblance of dwellers in the Warwicke Armes was clear. The Mason Bee lives in a community but not for it; she repels intrusion upon her own cell but shows no distress when that of her neighbor is raided or even destroyed; she does not love her neighbor; she stores no honey for the general treasure; and all her sweetness is spent upon herself.

Aurelia Hedge and the other ladies of the Warwicke Armes were unacquainted with the entomological studies of M. Fabre or they might have come upon his passage concerning the Mason Bee and improve the shining hour by meditation upon their greater

likeness to that individualist than to the more generous Little Busy Bee they had in mind. The further
conversation of Mrs. Hedge, this morning at breakfast, proved how little of her honey was for the in-
habitants of the other cells about her.

, "Of course they're all talking about it," she said
abruptly, after a pause.

"About bees?" her husband asked, a little surprised.

"No. Don't be such a dumb-bell! About our getting
left on the dump heap like this."

"Dump heap?" He looked up a little testily. "I
don't think much of that way of putting it, Aurelia.
I'm making just as good a living for you as I ever
did, I guess! We're no worse off than we were before,
are we? Just because Bill Greeley gets a rise I don't
see that we have to look at ourselves as being on the
dump heap."

"Don't you?"

"No, I certainly don't," he returned stoutly. "Bill
Greeley's made the best record in the business that
ever went on the N.K.U. books; he's actually a
commercial genius, and the Big Boss knows darn
well that the best thing the N.K.U. can do is to put
Bill way up. Bill's made good in every rise he's had

and, what is more, everybody in the whole N.K.U. likes him and pretty soon they'll all realize that he's entitled to this big lift to the top. Bill Greeley gets along with every man that's under him; he never puts on any airs with anybody, yet he knows how to make things hum! That's another reason the Big Boss has lifted him again and——"

Mrs. Hedge took the word from his mouth. "And passed him over your head!"

"Well, what of it? I haven't lost anything and Bill deserves it. I'm not demoted just because he's promoted, am I?"

"Aren't you?" she asked bitterly. "He's left you behind in the race, hasn't he? You got him his job with the N.K.U. and at first you had him under you. He passed you long ago; but from now on you and everybody else take his orders, don't you? He's got that to crow over, hasn't he?"

"Oh, look here!" Henry said; and he had become irritated. "Bill Greeley isn't crowing over anybody."

"Well, his wife is. Stella's crowing, isn't she?"

"I didn't see a sign of it when we talked to them last night—not in either of 'em. Naturally they're glad about it and she's proud of the showing Bill's made and delighted that the Big Boss appreciates his worth. Who wouldn't feel that way? I did myself. They're nice people and they're our best friends and I'm mighty glad to see them getting on in the world."

"At our expense?"

The irritation of Mr. Hedge was increased by this question. "Listen!" he said sharply. "It isn't at our expense or anybody else's expense. We're doing just as well as we ever did. My salary isn't lowered by Bill Greeley's getting lifted. You act to me like you just couldn't stand seeing friends of ours grow more prosperous than we are. Honestly, it seems to me like you're simply jealous, Aurelia."

She looked at him for a moment with the air of one too proud to make any defense against so low an accusation; then she rose and began to remove the breakfast dishes to the kitchenette. Her husband watched her gloomily; but, after a little while, went to a closet for his hat and prepared to depart for his place of business. At the door he paused.

"Honestly," he said, "that's how the way you act looks to me, Aurelia."

She made no reply other than that conveyed by a proud, hurt glance; then she turned her back to him, busying herself with the dishes. Upon this, Mr. Hedge sighed, opened his mouth to speak again, thought better of it and went forth. She turned sharply to the closed door.

"That's a nice idea to have of your wife!" she whispered fiercely.

But in truth Mr. Hedge's idea of his wife's emotion was not so far afield. To be surpassed by a protégé and to bear with grace such a surpassing, no small generosity of soul is needed; Aurelia Hedge was not gifted with that amount of generosity, and Stella Greeley had been her protégé. When the Greeleys, a younger couple and newly wedded, had come up from a small town, they had been in straits for a time until Henry Hedge, a distant cousin of the frightened bride, Stella, persuaded the National Kitchen Utensils factory manager to give young Greeley a trial in an unimportant position at a more unimportant salary. Aurelia had taken Stella under her wing and had kept her there during the years of the young husband's steady rise. The reversal of that position appeared unendurable; but it had to be faced, for now Greeley had been appointed factory manager and Henry Hedge was still an assistant in the "distribution department," the same position he had occupied when he brought his young friend into the business.

Aurelia was melancholy as she washed the dishes in the kitchenette sink. When the Hedges, followed obediently by the Greeleys, had moved into the new apartment house she had been a well satisfied young woman. She had regarded the Warwicke Armes as a "step up" in fashion and in luxury and in brightness of living. Moreover, this ascent had been accompanied by another: she had persuaded Henry to sell their hardy but cheap little automobile and to replace it with a "used sedan" of a more important appearance. In such a vehicle a lady living at the Warwicke Armes could be imagined as driving forth to tea at even the ponderous stone house of the Big Boss, Mr. Milton Cooper. Aurelia had daydreams, picturing herself in action among the important commercial personages who to her view moved upon the highest summit of the city's social range. Her indulgent fantasy reached its topmost pleasure when she imagined herself returned from one of Mrs. Milton Cooper's intimate dinners and sweeping into the Greeleys' beehive cell to tell Stella all about it.

The fantasy was benevolent toward the protégé. "When the gentlemen had gone into the marble smoking room for their coffee, I took Laura Cooper to one side and had a private talk with her." Aurelia

daydreamed on, continuing the imaginary narrative
to her friend. "I told her a lot of nice things about
you and Bill. 'Look here, Laura,' I said. 'The
Greeleys are regular people; they're really our own
kind. They've never seen the inside of your house.
Look here, Laura,' I told her, 'Stella Greeley is just
about the nicest little woman in the whole N.K.U.
outfit and she wouldn't be any more liable to commit
a social error in this house than you or I would ourselves. I absolutely know she'd be awf'ly congenial
and I'm going to bring her here to afternoon tea
to-morrow—just us three so you can get real ac-
quainted with her—and then you're going to ask
her to the very next one of these intimate small
dinners you give. I absolutely insist upon it, Laura!'
That's what I told her, Stella, and of course when I
put it that way she was perfectly sweet about it and
said if I liked you she knew she'd like you, too."

Pleasing fancies of this kind were no longer possible
for Aurelia; it was much more probable that the wife
of the new factory manager of the N.K.U. would
some day address Mrs. Cooper as "Laura" than that
Mrs. Henry Hedge ever would; and Aurelia's melancholy, this morning in her beehive cell, was not sweet-
ened by that realization. Her little friend Stella was

gay in the cell directly under foot; through the floor
of Aurelia's kitchenette there came faintly the sound
of jazz pulsated by radio. Stella was probably dancing
in and out of her own kitchenette just below.

"Upstart!" Aurelia murmured. Then she sighed
heavily as she thought of her husband and wondered
how it had ever come about that she was married
to a dull and plodding drudge.

II

AURELIA was unfortunate within herself. At thirty-four, a fresh colored small brunette, she had still a piquant prettiness of face; she was graceful and shapely, and she was mistress of the little personal art of dressing herself to display her shapeliness becomingly. She could drive an automobile; she danced well and cooked capably out of cans. She had not read a book of any kind for several years; newspapers bored her, except for their "Sunday supplements"; she sometimes bought a fashion magazine or one of the specialized periodicals concerned with motion pictures; but there her reading ended. A month before her wedding, when she was eighteen, she had graduated from the High School of the little town where she and Henry lived until they moved to the city; but Aurelia could not have passed any of the first-year examinations in that High School now. She had no interest at all in anything that affects general mankind unless she clearly saw how it affected herself: her mind was like a little

14

sand pile under a sieve; whatever was of any weight or size was rejected by the sieve and only the tiniest and most inconsequent particles came through. In the "supplements" she eagerly read the names of ladies who had subscribed for boxes at charity concerts, women probably never to be of her acquaintance; but for Aurelia columns concerned with war in China might as well have been printed in Chinese. So might political columns, scientific columns, musical columns, literary columns and columns devoted to history or discovery; Aurelia's eye glazed itself at sight of them and passed to "Beauty Hints." She spent several hours of every week at a "Beauty-Shoppe" where her dark hair was curled, her face kneaded, oiled and pinked, and every fingernail made into a rosy little mirror. She liked to see the tiny bright glistenings of her nails when she gestured, and was often preoccupied with them rather than with her cards when she played bridge. She took a lesson in bridge once a week but fatigued her mind with no other studies.

Sometimes she said she wished she could "find the time for French or music or something"; and she frequently complained that she was "rushed to death." Henry always lunched at the N.K.U. restaurant;

they dined three times a week at the cafeteria of the Warwicke Armes, and, on the evenings when they had dinner in their apartment, not much more than an hour was needed for the preparation of the meal, eating it and washing the dishes.

Henry used the trolley cars to go to the factory and return, leaving the sedan at the Warwicke Armes garage for Aurelia. Almost every morning she drove down town, left the car in a hired parking space, and walked to a department store, taking note of her reflection in all the plate glass show windows on the way. In the store, she might spend an hour pricing things and perhaps matching a shred of silk, buying a pair of stockings or a small vial of perfume or a box of scented powder. Then she would hurry to keep an engagement to lunch indigestibly with Stella Greeley at a confectioner's.

"My dear!" Aurelia would exclaim. "I'm half dead with shopping!" Then, if it didn't happen to be one of the days for hair dressing, manicuring and facial beautifying, they would go to the movies and stay until after five; and in the evening they would often persuade their husbands to take them to a movie theatre where there was dancing for the patrons.

Stella Greeley, four years younger, and following her leader's example—as she usually did in everything—formed the habit of saying, "I do wish I could find time to take French or music or something!"

III

STELLA'S radio was still loudly jazzing, that morning, when Aurelia came into the Greeleys' apartment; but Stella was no longer dancing in and out of the kitchenette, as her friend had correctly pictured her. Instead she sat at a dressing table, combing and brushing her short and wavy bright fair hair. The pale blue blouse and straw colored skirt she intended to wear lay upon a chair near by; and the fact that she wore no wrapper, in this interval of dressing, but sat before her mirror almost unclad, produced an effect somewhat irritating upon her friend.

Aurelia had long ago realized that this younger woman was beautiful "in a big blonde way"—thus Aurelia qualified the beauty and she frequently added another qualification by thinking of Mrs. Greeley as a "beautiful dumb-bell." The dumb-bell was not so dumb, however, as to be unaware of the beauty; indeed Stella was often provokingly fatuous about it, and this was not the first time Aurelia had found her enjoying a mirror's ample revelations of loveliness.

"Caught her at it again!" was the visitor's thought
—not quite a fair one, since Stella had voluntarily
stretched forth an arm to the door, close beside the
dressing table as soon as she recognized the voice
asking admittance. But her very willingness to be
"caught," so to speak, was productive of additional
irritation in Mrs. Hedge; it seemed to imply that
Stella's satisfaction with the mirror was visibly so
warranted that it would be shared by a female friend.
The female friend in question gave no outward sign
that it wasn't.

"Stella Greeley!" she exclaimed. "You certainly
are the most gorgeous looking thing in this town!
If I had just about a tenth of your looks I know
where I'd be!" She crossed the room, snapped off the
radio, and seated herself upon the maroon colored
sofa. "I wouldn't be living in any kitchenette apartment I tell you!"

"Wouldn't you?" Mrs. Greeley said, cheerfully interested. "Bill and I were talking that over last night
after you and Henry'd left. Bill asked me if I'd like
something bigger, or maybe a house out on the Boulevard, because he feels that now we can afford to spend
prob'ly about three times as much as we ever have
before; but I said, 'No. Let's not decide anything

like that in a hurry. Let's take our time,' I told him. 'We're comfortable enough the way it is and the Warwicke Armes is still good enough for us until we get our bearings and see what we really want to do.' Don't you think that's the sensible way to look at it, Aurelia?"

What Aurelia thought of that way of looking at it she was not so tactless as to say; for "Upstart!" was again the word in her mind. Already the Warwicke Armes was not good enough for the new factory manager and his wife, it seemed. A slight flush appeared upon Aurelia's forehead, though the lady before the mirror did not observe this token, nor, for that matter, would she have been able to interpret its meaning. Stella was of an amiable, credulous and simple turn of mind; she was usually cheerful, and now she was radiantly happy in the glow of her husband's success. Regarding Aurelia not only as her guide and counselor but as her dearest and most intimate friend, she had no perception that even from such a source some grudging and jealousy might be only natural under the circumstances.

"Don't you think that's the way to look at it, Aurelia," she repeated.

"Well——" Aurelia said, and paused. "Of course

in your new position you've got to consider yourself, Stella, and be careful not to take any false steps. Naturally things are liable to be pretty different between you and Bill from now on, you know, Stella."

The hairbrush in Stella's white and shapely hand ceased its movement, and for a moment came to rest upon her fair head; she was surprised. "Different between Bill and me? Why, how could that be?"

Aurelia laughed sadly; she sighed as if in pity for her friend's innocence. "It would be a lot better for you, dear, if you'd had more experience with men. You'd be better prepared for the way they act when they begin to get rich. You married too young, Stella, ever to really know much about them."

"But, goodness me! I certainly know all about Bill, Aurelia."

"Up to now you do, yes. But you've never known Bill with a big income and plenty of money in the bank to spend on anybody he likes to spend it on,"

Mrs. Greeley set the brush down on the table and turned to face her friend. "But, goodness me! You don't think Bill wants to spend——"

"You don't know men, dearie!"

Stella was puzzled and a little disturbed. "He's

never denied me anything I really wanted or needed; but you know how careful and saving he's always been. He doesn't care much about show and splurge. I'm sure that what he spends his money on will be something sensible, Aurelia."

"Yes," Mrs. Hedge said quickly. "But are you sure that *who* he spends it on will be something sensible?"

Stella's lovely blue eyes became larger in an astonished stare. "But who except me——"

Aurelia shook her head wisely and gloomily. "Rich men are subject to temptations that don't come other men's way."

"Yes; but of course Bill isn't rich yet and anyway——"

Aurelia interrupted with a little outcry of protest. "Don't say 'anyway,' Stella! You mean that 'anyway' he's too crazy about you. The devotion of a faithful wife never saved a man yet when a fascinating and designing woman got after him, and that's just the kind of women that do get after important men. The trouble with you and Bill is that he's become important. That's the whole trouble, Stella, and you certainly ought to see how careful you must be not to take a single false step at this juncture.

Just at this juncture, Stella, a single false step would be absolutely fatal."

Young Mrs. Greeley's expression, at first denoting mere puzzlement, had become a little perturbed. Nevertheless she laughed and seemed uninclined to be serious. "Why, Bill is the most faithful old soul in the world, and you've told me a hundred times, Aurelia, that you never did see a man that was crazier about his wife!"

"Yes—up to now."

"But, Aurelia——"

"Listen," Aurelia said, and the gravity with which she slowly shook her head checked the protest. "You don't know the workings of the N.K.U. like I do, Stella. I know the inner workings of the N.K.U. like a book. I knew everything that went on there long before Henry got 'em to give Bill a try. Bill is stepping into Joel Thomas's shoes as factory manager and Joel is retired at his own request. Do you know why, and do you know why George Peale, the factory manager before Joel Thomas, was also retired at his own request?"

"I don't know about Mr. Peale, Aurelia, and about Mr. Thomas I only know what Bill's told me. He said they'd given Mr. Thomas such large stock bonuses that with what he'd saved out of his salary he was well enough off to quit and buy a place in the country and travel and have a good time. Bill says Mr. Thomas has always wanted to take it easy and now he can. Isn't that why he quit?"

"It's anything *but !*" Aurelia said. "Thomas quit for the same reason Peale quit before him. He quit because his wife made him."

"Mrs. Thomas? What would she——"

"My, but you're dumb, Stella Greeley!" Aurelia cried. "You act as if you didn't know who was Peale's secretary and who was Thomas's secretary and who's going to be Bill's secretary now. She's been the N.K.U. factory manager's secretary for twelve years and she's still got the job, hasn't she?"

"What?" Stella said blankly, and her mystification seemed complete. "You don't mean to say you're talking about Miss Nelson?"

"Don't I?" Aurelia returned grimly. "Just you ask Mrs. Thomas whether I'm talking about Miss Nelson or not!"

Stella was unconvinced; she laughed. "Why, Miss Nelson must be at least thirty-eight!"

"Is that what she looks?"

"No; but she must be."

"Crystal Nelson's thirty-five," Mrs. Hedge said authoritatively. "She looks about twenty-three, and if you don't know yet that it's what a woman looks and not what she is that counts, it's time you found it out."

"Of course anybody knows that," Stella said, and, with a gentle unconsciousness that did not wholly please the caller, her glance returned to the mirror and remained there for several moments in a sweet placidity. "I think I can trust Bill perfectly, Aurelia," she added turning again toward Mrs. Hedge.

Aurelia felt baffled; she could not easily have explained why. She had not come down to her friend's apartment with the intention of making Stella jealous of Crystal Nelson; she had no such purpose, nor, so far as she was conscious, any purpose at all. Yet she found herself now—she knew not how—committed to a course of action seemingly founded upon precisely that purpose and that intention: it appeared necessary to convince Stella that Miss Nelson was a dangerous woman, inevitably threatening the marital peace of the Greeleys. The facts for the establishment of such a case against Miss Nelson were meager, and Aurelia had already overstated what had been merely gossip and rumor; but when she felt a pres-

sure to convince she had the habit of treating facts
as elastic conveniences to support argument. So now
she smiled pityingly and shook her head. "Mrs.
Peale was a pretty good-looking wife, too, Stella;
and Bill hasn't had any experience at all of women.
Have you ever seen a man yet that wouldn't fall for
an attractive woman's flattery? I don't envy you
what you may go through in the next few months,
Stella—I hate to say it; but indeed I do not!"

Again she was not without effect, and Mrs.
Greeley's expression became one of disquiet, although
she still offered resistance and protested. "But Bill's
always been so steady, Aurelia."

"Yes, and that's just the danger now. It's exactly that kind of man you've got to look out for
when some sudden success like this big new appointment comes his way. Men like that are the very
ones to lose their heads about women and go completely off the handle the minute they become important. You see, Stella, no woman has ever made any
fuss over Bill up to now. All this time he's been
plugging along in a subordinate position there wasn't
any reason to notice him. But now all at once he's
a big man out in the limelight, and you're going to

find things absolutely different: you'll have to watch him like a hawk."

"But how could I?" Stella returned plaintively. "I can't go down to the N.K.U. and sit in his office all day, can I?"

"No—and there's just the unfairness of it. That's what I hate worst about the whole thing, Stella. What I mean, it's the unfairness to women; we certainly get the raw end of the deal."

"How do you mean, Aurelia?" Mrs. Greeley asked, baffled by this abrupt generalization. "You mean if Miss Nelson tries to get Bill to flirting with her or——"

"I mean women don't get a square deal out of life, Stella. I mean, you take a woman for instance that's married a man when they were both pretty young, and lived with him through hard times when they were pinched and skimped for money, and done her share and worked with him to make both ends meet, and gone without good clothes and all the things she needed, and everything, so he could get ahead and make a career for himself—well, and suppose he *does* make a career for himself and all of a sudden begins to be looked on as a rich man, well, where does she stand *then?* That's what I mean by the unfairness of it."

"I don't see exactly, Aurelia. You mean——"

"I mean just what I say. You take a woman in that position, about our age, Stella, and I tell you she's got to look out for herself to keep from getting dished. Just *look* at the unfairness of it! Her husband's used to her; she's given the best years of her life to him; but so far as he's concerned she's just like some old shoe. And she isn't getting any *younger*, let me tell you! If he's going to dish her for some other woman, he may do it any day or he may put it off so long that it'll be too late for her to fix anything up for herself. That's the danger of it, Stella."

"You think——"

Mrs. Hedge did not permit this timorously begun question to be completed. "It's the danger of it, Stella," she interrupted, "and at the same time it's the unfairness of it. A man can be any age and he can look like the Old Scratch dressed up—it doesn't matter—if he's successful there'll always be women ready to jump at him. But here you take you and me, Stella, and we're just at the critical age. The way I look at it, if something happened to Henry and he began to make a whole lot of money all of a sudden,

I'd begin to take measures to protect myself. I'd begin to say to myself, 'Here! Look out! Right now I'm still attractive enough to land somebody else if he dishes me, and maybe a bigger fish than Henry at that! But a few years from now I won't be able to land anybody at all and *then* what'll I do if Henry dishes me? The only thing for me to do is to be ready to beat him to it! That's the way I feel, Stella, and I'm just passing it on to you because, looking at it one way, you're in that position right now."

"But Bill wouldn't ever——"

"Wouldn't he?" Aurelia asked quickly. "*Maybe* he wouldn't, Stella; but the point of it is that nobody on earth ever knows what a man will do if a clever woman gets hold of him." She paused, then suddenly and surprisingly laughed aloud. "But my goodness! If I had your shape and your face and your hair, I'd never worry about *that*, Stella Greeley! I'd certainly step out and show this town a few things if I had just about half of your advantages. I'd cut at least one swath for myself before they got *me* in the Old Ladies' Home!"

"Aurelia!"

"I certainly would!" Aurelia said, and she laughed again. "If I had your looks——"

Mrs. Greeley interrupted with conscientious modesty. "But I'm not a bit better looking than you are, Aurelia. In lots of ways I'm not half as——"

"Come off!" Aurelia said. "Let's get down to cases, as the men say. You know as well as I do who it was said you had eyes exactly the color of cornflowers. 'A beautiful woman with eyes exactly the color of cornflowers!' Wasn't that what he said just after you passed him at the last N.K.U. New Year's Day reception? The whole receiving line heard it, didn't they? He didn't say a thing about a single one of the other women there, and there were about three hundred of us. Don't pretend to be modest about it, Stella; you can't put any of that stuff over on me. I bet you've never looked in a mirror since the reception without thinking of the Big Boss's talking about your cornflower eyes!"

"I have, too!" Stella protested; but she blushed faintly and laughed. "I think Mr. Cooper's a nice man, and I'm certainly grateful to him for giving Bill this big promotion; but I don't believe——"

"You don't believe the cornflower eyes had anything to do with it," Aurelia interrupted archly; for now her manner had become rallying. "Of course not!"

"What!" And with this the cornflower eyes widened in complete astonishment. "Why, Aurelia Hedge!"

"Come off!" Mrs. Hedge said. "You don't mean to tell me you're as simple as that!"

"As what?"

"As not to put two and two together. When a man shows a thing that plainly, a woman's simply dumb if she doesn't know how to take advantage of it. When a man selects one woman out of three hundred to express his admiration about, and the very next big opening in his business goes to that same woman's husband——"

"Aurelia! Why, that's ridiculous. Bill's promotion has come through his own——"

"Pooh!" Aurelia said boldly. "Cooper's got a dozen men at the N.K.U. just as able as Bill and with more experience."

"But I don't think it's fair to Bill for anyone to say——"

"To say that he isn't the first man to be helped by his wife's pretty eyes?" Aurelia interposed gaily; and she noted that her friend's blush had deepened. "All right, I won't say it then." But at the archness of her glance, Stella cried out.

"Aurelia Hedge, you're a perfect goose! Mr. Cooper wouldn't know me again if he saw me."

"Oh, wouldn't he though!"

"Not unless I was with Bill. And besides that, everybody says he's always been absolutely devoted to Mrs. Cooper."

"Yes," Aurelia said, becoming serious again;— "and so's Henry Hedge devoted to me. But if Henry was going to have Crystal Nelson for his secretary— well, I'd begin to wonder a little where *I* was going to *stand*, maybe, before long. That'd be *my* state of mind, Stella; but I think I'd know how to turn the tables all right if I stood in *your* shoes. I tell you if I had your advantages, Stella Greeley——"

"No, you wouldn't," Stella said, and she jumped up abruptly and began to complete her dressing. "You'd stick to your old Henry just as I'd stick to my old Bill. What nonsense we're talking! How'd we ever happen to begin it? I want to hop downtown and get a manicure. You going with me?"

"Yes," Aurelia answered. "My nails are dreadful. If Mr. Cooper gives a party in honor of the new factory manager, the way he did when he appointed Mr. Thomas, what you going to wear, Stella? You better work Bill for enough to get something in cornflower colored chiffon."

"Oh, you big goose!" Stella cried. "You quit teasing me! He wouldn't know whether I wore cornflower colored chiffon or corn-sack colored denim."

"Who?" Aurelia inquired slyly. "Bill?"

"Oh, you crazy cut-up!" And upon that, both of them began to laugh loudly, as if with the impetus of something at once daring and ridiculous. Then, when their laughter died down, the subject of their discourse became less intimately personal, being concerned with party clothes in general, and presently they were on their way in Aurelia's sedan still thus preoccupied. But as they descended from the car, Stella said absently, without prelude, or any apparent connection of idea:

"You big goose! I bet he's over fifty years old!"

"Who?" Aurelia asked again. "Bill?" And in a gale of renewed laughter they entered the manicurist's shop.

IV

AT THE banquet celebrating the inauguration
of the new factory manager with whose in-
cumbency the "new policy" of the N.K.U.
began, it was both befitting and complimentary that
Mrs. William Greeley, wife of the new manager, sat
upon the right of Mr. Milton Cooper, president
of the corporation and donor of the feast. No one
could more becomingly have adorned so conspicuous
a position of honor; and Stella, faintly blushing, in
scanty cornflower colored chiffon, was thought charming by almost all of the eight hundred people present.

The banquet room was vast, for it was the Audi-
torium Chamber of the N.K.U. and two thousand
sometimes sat there to hear a concert or a lecture or
to watch an educational movie; but to-night the great
canopy of blue had been lowered, shutting off the
galleries and forming a temporary ceiling. Innumera-
ble stars of thin nickel sparkled down from it; there
was a silver-plated vase of six pink roses upon every
one of the small tables at which most of the banquet-

ers sat; and the N.K.U. band, in uniform, glittered
at the end of the room opposite the Speakers' Table,
which was slightly elevated upon a long dais. Here,
thus visibly eminent, the grandees of the occasion
sat emphasized against a background of green fronds
drooping from a grove of palm trees; the cloth was
white damask and upon it were ten vases; but here
every vase was the silver fountain-mouth for an
unfalling spray of two dozen pink roses. The spray
was a match for Stella's cheeks; her hair shone against
the green behind her like the gold coronal of a queen
in a tapestry; she sat with downcast eyes, knowing
that all of the women in the place—and most of the
men, too, except during intervals of eating—were
looking at her and thinking and talking about her.

Mrs. Henry Hedge, at a table for eight midway
down the vast room, talked of nothing else. "Scared
to death!" she informed her neighbors eagerly. "I
been grooming her for it all day. 'Look here, Stella'!
I told her, the last thing before I put her in my car
to bring her here. '*You* don't have to make a speech,'
I told her. 'All you have to do is *sit* there,' I said.
But after all, who wouldn't be scared? Of course nobody dreamed Mr. Cooper ever meant to make such
a tremendous event of it. When Mr. Thomas and

Mr. Peale were appointed, it certainly wasn't anything like *this!* You know that, yourself, Mrs. Royce."

Aurelia had the benevolent attention of the whole table but addressed herself particularly to a stout lady in blue velvet seated opposite her. Mrs. Royce was consort to the Manager of the Central Sales Department and officially, so to speak, the most important person of the group. She nodded affably. "Of course it's partly because Mr. Cooper wants to rouse enthusiasm for the New Policy; but it's a big tribute to what he thinks of Mr. Greeley. Besides, I must say Mrs. Greeley looks a perfect queen—kind of like a queen from some foreign country being entertained by a king and sharing his throne for the evening." Mrs. Royce paused to titter, half apologetically, half approvingly, to ameliorate so daring a flight of fancy. "Mrs. Greeley's an intimate friend of yours, Mrs. Hedge?"

"'Intimate'?" Aurelia cried. "I brought her up! She's about my age, of course; but she's a near relation of Mr. Hedge's and they've been under our wing, as you may say, ever since they came to town. Mr. Hedge put Bill Greeley into the N.K.U. and has pushed him as fast as he could ever since. As for

Stella——" Here Aurelia paused, glanced toward
the royal platform and uttered a little cry of petulant
distress. "Oh, dear! She has a habit of holding her
head on one side that isn't becoming. I *told* her not
to do that to-night; but she's so rattled she's absolutely forgotten! Oh, dear me, I *wish*, she wouldn't
do it! I wish I had some way of getting word to her."
Increasingly troubled, Aurelia made sounds of lam-
entation, then, as if inspired by a bright thought,
appealed to a comely, dark eyed young woman who
sat at the head of this table. "Miss Nelson, *do*
you think there's any way for me to get a message
sent up to the Speakers' Table?"

Miss Nelson seemed not to hear. She had other
matters in hand, and after listening to the earlier
part of Aurelia's discourse and perceiving that it
was only a familiar commonplace of the N.K.U.
social establishment—a claim to possessive intimacy
with new-made grandees—she had closed her ears to
the excited and intentionally elegant tones of Mrs.
Hedge's voice. This withdrawal of attention on Miss
Nelson's part, however, was not for the purpose of
conversing with her next neighbors at the table. A
stout, bald man of anxious countenance, the caterer,
came from time to time for a whispered word with

her; she listened silently and dismissed him with a decisive nod or a monosyllable; sometimes she wrote briefly upon a slip of paper and gave it to a waiter stationed near her; he carried it quickly away, and all the while her capable and intelligent eyes quietly took note of everything in every part of the room.

A corner of the suspended blue canopy sagged unduly; Miss Nelson gave the waiter a word on paper, and almost immediately the drooping cloth rose into place, elevated by unseen powers above. She nodded to the waiter, a gesture unnoticed by anyone except himself, and within the moment the gorgeous leader of the N.K.U. band clicked his metal easel with a baton and music, brazenly dulcet, swam upon sixteen hundred ears. And yet so quietly and so quickly were Miss Crystal Nelson's decisions made and her signals given that not a man and not even a woman at her own table guessed that she sat at this great feast like a commander-in-chief in his headquarters, master of every event and movement. Aurelia appealed to her with no idea except to expand the audience that was being impressed by her anxiety to correct the posture of her protégé's lead.

She repeated the appeal in a louder and shriller

voice. "Miss Nelson, *do* you think there's any way I could get a message up to Stell'?"

"Stell?" Miss Nelson said inquiringly. "I don't know any Mr. Stell. Where is he?"

Henry Hedge, across the table from his wife, laughed gloomily in the manner of a husband confirmed in the conviction that his wife is making herself ridiculous, but Aurelia spared him only the briefest glance, promising him something for this, later, and explained loudly to Miss Nelson:

"No, no! I mean Stella Greeley. She absolutely promised me she *wouldn't* sit with her head on one side the way she is now—it's a habit she's got as I was just saying to Mrs. Royce—but she's so rattled she's forgotten more than half of what I told her! What I wondered: *Do* you suppose there's any way I could get word up to the Speakers' Table to tell her to quit sitting that way before Mr. Cooper notices?" Aurelia interrupted herself to laugh excitedly. "Oh, dear! If she just *would* straighten her head up and not sit all sort of bunched that way! I told her not to five hundred times!"

"I'd just been thinking," Miss Nelson returned, "that Mrs. Greeley's attitude was one of remarkable gracefulness."

Aurelia cried out shrilly, protesting. "Oh, my! Not close up to her, Miss Nelson! It may look graceful to you from this long distance away; but if you were sitting right next to her like Mr. Cooper is, you'd see that it gives her a bunched up look. I'm *so* anxious to get word to her to sit up straight before he turns from talking to the Mayor and notices Stell'. Really, I'll just die if she doesn't snap out o' that before he starts talking to her!"

Aurelia spoke with an accompaniment of fluttering gestures; her hands, head and shoulders moved constantly to emphasize her meaning; and, that none of it might be lost, so did her face continually move in the last extremes of expressiveness. Crystal Nelson looked at her thoughtfully before responding.

"I don't believe you need worry, Mrs. Hedge. Mr. Cooper surely won't think uncharitably of Mrs. Greeley even if——"

"Good gracious, Miss Nelson! Everybody knows how much any man in the N.K.U. depends on the impression at headquarters about his wife. I mean of course his wife and his——"

"And his family life." Miss Nelson took her up. "Yes, certainly it's generally understood that Mr. Cooper takes a great interest in the family life of all of us because he believes that everybody's efficiency depends a lot on domestic surroundings, 'helpful influence in the home' and all that. I don't think Mr. Greeley would be injured with him because Mrs. Greeley holds her head becomingly—or unbecomingly, if you like—on one side."

"Don't you?" Aurelia uttered a loud titter, and, in her excitement, became a little reckless. A curious but not uncommon thing had happened to her. Since her first talk with Stella, on the morning after the promotion of the latter's husband, when Aurelia, almost not knowing why, had begun to disturb her beautiful friend's complacency with fears of Miss Nelson and strange hopes of Mr. Cooper, the new topics had been intermittently but persistently an undercurrent in the daily intercourse of the two ladies of the Warwicke Armes. So constant a thought, no matter how flimsy its origin or how well known its flimsiness is to its projector, must ever and ever gain in substantiality to even that very projector; thus Aurelia herself now took it for something at least approaching reality.

Moreover, the jealousy she had of Stella's rise in life was becoming subsidiary to the ambition to find importance in being the proprietor, so to speak, of so

important a person. This proprietorship, which she
was virtually proclaiming to her neighbors at the
banquet, seemed to her to be made light of—in fact
almost ridiculed—by the cool and examining gaze, as
well as the rather dry tone of voice, of Miss Crystal
Nelson. Irritated, Aurelia felt herself challenged;
her impulse therefore was to make the importance
of her proprietorship of Stella more pronounced;
and she was further goaded by another gloomy laugh
from her husband, who had evidently become somewhat rash about what would happen to him later.
She assumed the arch knowing air of a person privy
to spicy high matters obscure to others, and let her
voice become almost obviously derisive. "I expect
you haven't noticed anything different between
this affair and what happened when Mr. Peale and
Mr. Thomas got *their* appointments."

"What difference do you mean, Mrs. Hedge?"

"What difference?" Aurelia laughed merrily.
"Good gracious me, Miss Nelson, use your eyes!"
And then, as the use to which Miss Nelson put her
fine dark eyes remained a thoughtful contemplation
of the lady addressing her, the latter made a roguish
movement of her head toward the Speakers' Table.
"You're looking in the wrong direction!" she

cried. "Did you notice any orchids when Mr. Peale or Mr. Thomas got appointed to the managership?"

The only orchids visible, delicately exotic against cornflower blue, were upon Stella's breast. Aurelia thus made her point sufficiently plain to the three other women at her own table, though the four men had no idea of what she was really saying, and even her husband only thought dismally that she was too noisily "showing off" her intimacy with Stella. But Aurelia was becoming a little intoxicated with her own daring and gayety as well as with what she felt was the dramatic quality of the occasion. The brilliancy of the banquet and the music of the band had gone to her head; she felt, too, that she held the keys, as a playwright might say, to a tremendous situation; and she was pleased to think that she was now triumphing in superior knowingness over Miss Nelson, whom she naturally disliked for always seeming, as Aurelia had complained to confidantes, "so smart aleck mysterious!"

Miss Nelson remained mysterious now, at least so far as any revelation of her thoughts concerning orchids went; she said nothing and Aurelia turned to Mrs. Royce. "You never saw anybody worse rattled in your life!" she said. "Honestly, when those orchids came this afternoon I thought Stell' would throw a fit! There was a card 'Congratulations and best wishes of the N.K.U.' but of course she couldn't *help* knowing who sent 'em!"

Mrs. Royce was interested but skeptical. "Do you think so, Mrs. Hedge? Do you suppose Mr. Cooper attends to details like that himself? I always thought he just gave general directions and the details were carried out by someone on the staff."

"Oh, yes, generally," Aurelia admitted. "But in *this* case——" She concluded the implication not in words but with a murmur of laughter and a toss of the head. "Poor Mrs. Thomas and Mrs. Peale!" she added. "*They* weren't sent any——" and again she left a sentence unfinished except by her knowing laughter. Then she assumed an air of gravity and seemed to become solicitous. "Mrs. Royce, have you heard how Mrs. Cooper was to-day?"

"To-day?" Mrs. Royce repeated, evidently surprised. "Why, no; I didn't know she was that sick. Of course I'd heard she had the flu; but everybody said she was getting along all right. I heard she'd probably be out in a few days."

Aurelia seemed to be almost shocked by this lack

of information. "Oh, no!" she said. "No, indeed! Flu does lead into the most terrible complications. You'd think the doctors would have learned by this time how to stop 'em; but they haven't." For a moment she appeared to be depressed by this thought; then she brightened. "Wouldn't it be curious if——" She paused, glanced as though unconsciously toward the two central figures at the Speakers' Table, laughed excitedly and concluded: "Well, I guess I'd better not say *that!*"

Mrs. Royce was evidently able to follow the thought whether it was spoken or not. "My goodness, Mrs. Hedge!" she exclaimed admiringly. "You certainly are a cut-up!" She leaned forward, lowering her voice after the manner of ladies engaged with secret imports. "You aren't serious? You don't really mean——"

Mrs. Hedge nodded triumphantly, "Yes, I do!"

"Well, I declare!" Mrs. Royce leaned back in her chair and gazed at the Speakers' Table. "I hadn't heard a word of it." She turned again toward Aurelia. "My goodness! You never can tell, can you?"

"*I* can," Aurelia returned quickly. "Anyhow in *this* case."

Here Mrs. Royce's husband, sitting next to Aurelia,

intervened. "What on earth are you two talking about? Let the rest of us in on it, won't you?"

They paid no attention to him but gave heed to Mrs. Caples, the fourth lady at the table. She leaned toward Aurelia eagerly; "Say! How long has it been going on?"

But Miss Nelson, a moment before, had whispered hurriedly to the waiter in special attendance, and now the band blared forth "The Washington Post" with a vigor that abruptly stopped every conversation in the room. During this interlude Mrs. Royce and Mrs. Caples stared absorbedly at the distant Stella Greeley, glorified to them, albeit with a tinge of scarlet by the information they had just received. Information surely of import since it came from Mrs. Greeley's bosom friend.

V

WHEN the brazen jubilations of the overwhelming band ceased from uproar, Mr. Royce finished the small cup of black coffee that had been set before him, and returned to his inquiry. "Put us poor, dumb old men wise, Mrs. Hedge. What you ladies been stirrin' up? Of course I know my wife'll tell me to-night when we get home, and once her and Mrs. Caples know what it is, it'll be all out among the N.K.U. ladies to-morrow; but what's the matter our hearin' about it now? Caples, you help me make 'em come through."

Mr. Caples, a heavy man, had been paying more attention to the food than to the talk of the women. "Make 'em come through with what?"

"With whatever scandal they've got themselves all worked up over," Mr. Royce returned humorously. "They've nosed out something pretty good; I know that much, and I don't want to haf to wait till we're undressing to go to bed for Mrs. Royce to tell me, because by that time I'm always too sleepy to take any big interest in it—that's the way she does. Caples, you get her to tell it to you now, and I'll tackle Mrs. Hedge here. She started it and I guess she certainly knows all."

Miss Nelson lightly tapped a spoon upon her coffee cup. "*Sh!* Mr. Cooper is rising. The speeches are going to begin."

As a matter of precise fact, Mr. Cooper was not in the act of rising at the moment when she said he was; instead he was coughing slightly and looking at the palm of his right hand. Miss Nelson's statement, therefore, must have been in the nature of a prediction, for which she had good ground, however. Mr. Cooper's coughing was of the kind always a prelude to oratory, and what he looked at, in his hand, was a slip of paper inscribed in pencil:

"Have instructed waiters not to clear until the speeches are over. Would begin as soon as possible after band stops.

"C. N."

Mr. Cooper crumpled the paper, finished his coughing, rose and struck the table one sharp blow with a silver gavel. Instantly, everywhere in the assemblage, there was silence, for all of the guests at the banquet

except the Mayor and a few deferential others at the
Speakers' Table, beheld before them the master of
their destinies, the dispenser of fortune, the center of
hope and the cause of fear. Mr. Milton Cooper dis-
played no inadequate figure for such a part: at fifty
he had no gray hair, no dubious teeth; he spent more
time upon a horse's back than in a motor car, was
broad at the shoulders, flat at the waist; and from his
tanned dark face the enthusiast's bright eyes pro-
jected the sparkle of a fanaticism still vehement.
The N.K.U. was his deity as it had been that of his
father, the founder, before him.

Moreover, since he thought of himself as its oracle,
his own edicts appeared, even to himself, to issue
from a higher power, and so became august and unal-
terable. Nevertheless, he was in this at times a little
inconsistent, for he had a habit of using "N.K.U."
and the pronoun "I" as synonyms perfectly inter-
changeable. Thus, addressing his banqueters in a
high, resonant voice, he said:

"The N.K.U. wishes that every one of its employees could have been here with us to-night; but
for various reasons I found it more feasible to invite
only you who are the upper tenth of them. The
N.K.U. trusts you to distribute the meaning of my

remarks to all those under you, so that I may be confident that no one whatever can misunderstand the New Policy of the N.K.U. The N.K.U. seizes the occasion of inaugurating a new factory manager to make clear this policy and the N.K.U. will now set it before you in such plain language that I think you will all comprehend me."

His description of the "New Policy" was as lucid as he promised; it could not affect the workmen in the several great factories of the N.K.U. for they were protected from it, so to speak, by their unions; but it did apply incitingly and threateningly to the subchieftains and assistants now banqueting in presence of the oracle. Emulating the Navy and the Army, the N.K.U. had devised a system of Promotion Marks that would determine the relative positions of all these servitors of the institution. For every year of his service—"and by that I mean service satisfactory to the N.K.U.," Mr. Cooper explained— every man would receive, not a promotion but a Promotion Mark. And that the balance of justice might be maintained any failure in duty, or any slackness, or inefficiency would entail the loss of a Promotion Mark.

"These Promotion Marks, these barometers of

your loyalty to the N.K.U.," he went on, "will be constantly watched by the N.K.U. and I assure you, from the highest down to the lowest, from our splendid new factory manager down to the youngest clerk in the N.K.U. chain of hardware stores, your absolute value to this institution will be a matter of visible black on white. When there is a question of promotion or demotion the N.K.U. has only to consult the ledger containing the registry of your marks. You see what this means: with a sufficient number of Promotion Marks a man may rise rapidly from a lower department to a higher; he may be lifted from behind the counter of one of our chain stores in a village and brought here into one of our headquarters departments, so that not only would he receive the higher salary but he and his family would enjoy the advantages and comforts of life in the city, instead of the more limited opportunities of the small town. You see what a splendid vista of success is thus opened to the ambition of every man who employs his best brains and energy toward the forwarding of this great industrial institution."

Most of his hearers, comprehending something more than he said, perceived not only the pleasant vista he mentioned but the other necessarily opening

before them if they failed to use their best brains
and energy toward the forwarding of the great
industrial institution. They looked serious and the
seriousness of many of them became anxiety as their
overlord went on with his explanation. The New
Policy was retroactive, he said, and for months the
N.K.U. had been quietly busy upon the fateful
ledger of marks. A Promotion Mark had already been
awarded to every man for every past year of service
deemed satisfactory by the N.K.U. The N.K.U.,
however, reserved to itself sole access to the records,
since the New Policy was still an experiment. Later,
the N.K.U. might think it wiser to conduct the ledger
as an open bulletin, where every man might find his
own marks and those of all his competitors in service; but for the present the ledger was reserved for
the information of the N.K.U. alone. Already that
information had been of great use to the N.K.U. and
the N.K.U. would constantly act upon it.

At that, even the cheerful and honest face of the
new factory manager became grave; but to the new
manager's wife all this talk about marks was
mere sound. Dazzled by herself, Stella sat in what
was almost a stupor of ecstatic self-consciousness.
About her enthronement it seemed to her that

there was a radiation of golden light, illuminating her and yet emanating from her.

Outside of this light and beyond the encasement of her self-consciousness the rest of the world seemed to consist of admiring eyes bent wonderingly upon her; and only the meaning of what directly and obviously concerned herself reached her intelligence. All evening heavenly phrases had been picking themselves out of the noisy jumble of the banqueters' voices and sounding little exquisite strains of music within her ears. Over and over she had heard two words coupled in strongest emphasis: "*Some peach!*" And even oftener, when she heard the hearty exclamations, "*I'll* say she is" and "*I'll* tell the cock-eyed world!" she felt that golden light about her brightening and brightening.

It seemed to her that until Bill's promotion the world had been like a dark theatre in which she sat obscurely contented with her obscurity and not even aware that before her was a curtain about to rise. It had risen, disclosing a commotion of dancers in a palace garden, a rich and beautiful spectacle but dim at the very first because the lights were not instantly full; yet every moment they had grown brighter and the shapes of the dancers more distinguishable until, quickly enough, she saw that there was one startlingly beautiful figure about which all the other shining figures tossed and whirled, and that it was her own.

This glamorous ballot, so largely the production of that instinctive impresario, Aurelia Hedge, had no lack of drama. Among the lively figures on the stage of Stella's imagination was that of Aurelia herself, playing the bright-eyed little confidante, bosom friend to the heroine, ready with aid against the darker figures; for of necessity there must be villains. These were still a little vaguely villainous it is true, in the heroine's mind; they existed there, however, as powers in opposition, increasingly distasteful, and were represented by the figures of her husband and Crystal Nelson—the latter thus far only a disliked shadow, for Stella had never seen the capable Miss Nelson. Finally, in the foreground of the spectacle and next in brightness to the star herself, there moved a glittering, powerful shape, the semblance of Mr. Milton Cooper. The postures of this important figure expressed always a dignified yet passionate admiration, and thus, continuously personifying a single motion was perhaps more marionette than human.

Moreover, when the actual Milton Cooper engaged himself in matters outside the marionettish rôle arranged for him in Stella's ballet drama, he virtually ceased to exist, so far as she was concerned, until he came back to it again. So now, as he went on with his explanation of Promotion Marks and the New Policy his voice seemed to be little more than a distant whirring of factory machinery; but with a change in his theme she began to listen attentively.

"The N.K.U. depends upon the wife of every loyal man in the N.K.U. forces," Mr. Cooper said vehemently, "to second and further her husband's efforts to set good marks beside his name on the records. As you know, the N.K.U. takes the most earnest interest in the domestic relations of every man employed, and that is because the N.K.U. feels that nobody can give his best effort unless that effort is supported, heart and soul, from the home. You wives who are here to-night can do more than see that your hearths are swept and your tablecloths spotless; you can stimulate your husbands' ambition, you can *make* them forge ahead. I will be personal—the N.K.U. is really one big family, and, since we are talking in the family circle, such allusion is allowable

—so I am going to ask you to look for a moment at the lady seated upon my right."

He paused, and Stella, blushing exquisitely, felt her heart fluttering with a delicious stage fright. Everyone knew that the Big Boss was about to pay her a tremendous compliment, and there was a general murmur of approbation that culminated in a single outstanding squeal of excitement from a table near the center of the room. All of the banqueters looked benevolent, the gentlemen especially so; but probably some of the ladies were inwardly a little cynical. These were not inimical, however; their cynicism was tolerant, for almost all women learn early to bear with the simplicity of a man who takes a woman's beauty as proof enough that she is everything he believes specially admirable. All in all, there was a multitudinous beaming upon the blushing lady at Mr. Cooper's right.

"With such a helpmate," he said gallantly, "could any man fail to reach the pinnacle? With such encouragement ever stimulating his efforts and with a loyal smile from so gracious a source waiting to greet him in the home after each day's industry, could any man falter in his path toward the goal? I think not. I think not, my friends. No, the N.K.U.

depends as much upon the home behind the man as it does upon the man himself, and to express this sentiment I take great pleasure in calling upon one of the N.K.U.'s most devoted friends, His Honor, the Mayor of our beautiful city, who will give you, in his own inimitable manner, a toast—to the ladies!"

The Mayor arose, blandly waggish. "Mr. Chairman, ladies and gentlemen," he said; "I am familiar of course with the interest this great institution has always taken in the domestic felicity of its employees; but I profess that never before to-night had I considered you, Mr. Chairman, a susceptible man. I had, in fact, thought of you quite otherwise, and as distinctly the opposite; but to-night I see that I was wrong, and in this fair presence—" here he paused and bowed to Stella—"in this fair presence I not only comprehend but share, sir, in your susceptibility!"

Laughter and heavy applause attended this sally, and the pleased chairman said loudly, "Perfectly true! Perfectly true!" Stella blushed even more deeply, then the downcast thick lashes over her brilliant eyes rose; she gave Mr. Cooper a quick, shining look and almost instantly veiled it. The Mayor went on with his speech; and, although his theme became more general, concerning itself with "divine womanhood," it nevertheless seemed still to be personal to her, and so did that of the speaker who followed him. Following this lead, the third orator opened his address with a knightly bow to her and the words, "To this fair presence—nay, more to this inspiring presence—I bring my own humble garland." After he had finished, his successor paid her a similar tribute, though his was somewhat more florid: "I yield to no man," he said, "in my fealty to the fair sex, and when I rise to speak in the presence of the fairest of that sex, let me tell you that I also yield to no man in my envy of the proud husband now being inducted into the factory managership of this vast institution."

He was warmly applauded by the men and indulgently by the women; though no doubt some of the latter felt that these distinguished gentlemen at the Speakers' Table were making geese of themselves, in the manner of men (especially middle-aged and elderly men) over a pretty woman. Nevertheless, it was Stella's great night, not her husband's: the banquet was supposedly in his honor (with the New Policy of course as a submotive) but the only refer-

ence to him made by any of the invited orators was
the allusion to him as a "proud husband." And when
his own turn came to speak, at the end of the program, he produced in perfection an example of the
effect known as anti-climax.

He made two things clear to every person in his
audience: that he had no talent for public speaking
and that he was suffering piteously from stage fright.
His broad and kindly face was pale and bedewed;
his voice shook and so, too visibly, did the hand with
which he was once or twice unfortunately inspired to
attempt a gesture. What he said failed to kindle enthusiasm, for, in substance, it was that although he
felt far from sure of possessing the ability to fill the
position to which Mr. Cooper had so generously
and surprisingly appointed him, and although there
were probably many other men in the N.K.U.
service who could fill the position as well, or better,
he would go ahead gratefully and try his best to be a
good factory manager.

Then, having set forth this resolution in a feeble
voice, he sat down with the evident relief of a man
who has gone through a horrible experience and unexpectedly come out at least alive; the band burst
out with the "Star Spangled Banner" and the great

company of people rose with unanimous patriotic alacrity.

With the performance of this ceremony the banquet ended, though a reception in honor of the new factory manager was to follow in an adjoining lobby, and when the music stopped, William Greeley left his place at one end of the Speakers' Table and came through the grove of palms, behind the table, to join his wife. He had recovered his customary good spirits, though he was still wiping his brow.

"Well, honey," he said, chuckling happily, "I got through it somehow and I didn't get shot!"

But Stella had just taken the proffered arm of the president of the N.K.U. to proceed to the lobby; she leaned behind her escort's back, and, in a chilling whisper, responded to her husband thus:

"You ought to've been!"

Then, readjusting the expression of her face to an amiable aspect, she swept grandly away upon Mr. Cooper's arm. Rueful, William tagged along after them and presently took his place beside them in the lobby to shake hands with the long files of people coming from the banquet tables. But here, as at the banquet, his position was that of a subordinate personage; it was still Stella's night and not his. She and the Big Boss were the center of a happy commotion that seemed to leave William outside. Stella was more radiant than ever; Aurelia gasped out a whisper in her ear, "You've *got* it!" as she and the patient Henry came by her. Stella gave her friend a delirious pinch on the arm, and then, as Aurelia whispered, "Look who's behind me!" offered to view a temporary but decisive change of demeanor.

The next person in line behind Aurelia was Miss Crystal Nelson; Stella saw her for the first time, but understood Aurelia perfectly. Miss Nelson looked friendly and extended a slender hand: "I'm Crystal Nelson, Mrs. Greeley," she said. "I hope——"

"No doubt you do," Stella interrupted, and, seeming not to see Miss Nelson's hand, heartily shook that of Mrs. Caples who followed next, and began to chatter cordially to her. She was exuberant with Mrs. Caples, indeed; her voice was loud in this exuberance for she caught the admiring backward glance of Aurelia and felt the tense exhilaration that comes sometimes to a woman who snubs and finds the proper audience to applaud her.

VI

FOR the Greeleys and Hedges so glorious an evening could not be concluded by merely going home and to bed. Arrived at the Warwicke Armes, however, the quartette immediately separated itself into duets, Stella and Aurelia ascending to the latter's apartment for theirs, while Mr. Greeley and Mr. Hedge disposed themselves for conversational reminiscence in the quarters soon to be vacated by the Greeleys. Henry Hedge removed his coat and hung it carefully upon the back of a chair.

"I never do feel just comfortable in a tuck," he explained. "Besides, I want to make this one last out my days. It isn't everybody that's got the money to sling around as easy as you're going to be able to, Bill."

Then, as both gentlemen seated themselves near the radiator and propped their feet upon its gilt coils, he added, "Well, it certainly was a great night for Stella, Bill. She certainly looked her best."

"She certainly did," his friend agreed, then laughed and groaned. "Oh, my! I certainly cut a fine figure as an orator! Stella said afterwards I ought to've been shot and she never was righter in her life. Honestly, Henry, when I got on my feet I didn't think I was going to live through it and I don't know how I did. I guess I was just about the limit, wasn't I? In confidence, now, Henry, was I really as terrible as I sounded to myself, do you think? Did you ever hear a worse speech in your life, or didn't you?"

Mr. Hedge turned toward him the melancholy but kindly face of a true friend. "Well, I don't know as it did you any harm, Bill; and anyhow a man as good as you are in the business doesn't need to be such an all-fired grand speech maker. Your voice was so low and shaky, and Aurelia was fluttering around and whispering so much at our table—showing off about how thick she is with Stella and all—I couldn't get much more than about one fourth of what you said. The gist of it seemed to be that you were a mighty poor man for the place; but, as I say, it isn't going to do you any harm to be the one that says that. No, Bill, *that* won't do you any harm."

"I hope not," William said doubtfully. Then, sighing gently, he glanced about the little apartment.

"Henry, this has been a right cosy little place to live in and it's been pleasant being in the same building with you and Aurelia. I'll hate to leave it; but of course you see how it is: we had to recognize the fact that the Big Boss would naturally want us to live up to the job in outward appearances as well as every other way, and Stella got crazy for a house, too, so of course——"

"Of course," Mr. Hedge agreed sympathetically. "You'll get to enjoy it, Bill, after a while, too; you'll get used to living in a big house. And anyhow *that* isn't going to do you any harm, Bill."

The new factory manager moaned jocosely. "No, I expect if that speech of mine to-night didn't do me any harm why nothing else on earth could!"

"Your speech?" Mr. Hedge said, and he looked frowningly at the cigar he was smoking. "No, *that* isn't going to do you any harm, Bill."

Something in the tone of this repetition, and the emphasis Mr. Hedge put upon the word "that," caught his friend's inquiring attention. "Something's on your mind, Henry. What is it that is going to do me some harm?"

"Oh, nothing—nothing at all. I was only think-ing——"

"You worrying about the New Policy—those Promotion Marks, Henry?"

"I guess we've all got to worry about them some; but no, Bill, that wasn't what I was thinking about."

"Well, what were you thinking about?"

Mr. Hedge took his time. "Well, it wasn't much," he said slowly. "Fact is, I might have been mistaken. Anyway, it was just a little thing and probably won't ever amount to enough to take notice of. It was something that happened at the reception, and you were standing right there; you probably saw what it was yourself."

"No, I didn't. Was it anything the Big Boss——"

"No, and I'm pretty sure he didn't notice it. That is, he didn't notice it this time. But it was one of those kind of things that if they happen once are pretty likely to go on happening, and some other time he probably would notice it and it might make him think you were getting the big head, Bill. Fact is, it might make everybody think so; and you know yourself that to have a lot of talk going around about how you are getting the big head wouldn't do you any good, Bill."

"Me?" William Greeley's feet slid down from the

radiator and struck the floor with a thump. "Why, how on earth could anybody ever——"

"Nobody that knows you right well would think such a thing, Bill," Mr. Hedge said gently. "But of course you know how it is: when a man's wife shows signs of big head everybody thinks they've both got it and——"

"You mean you noticed Stella doing something that might make people say——"

"Well, it was hardly anything, Bill. It was just a symptom, so to speak—something maybe you ought to warn her to look out for, so it wouldn't get to growing on her, as it were. Unpopularity begins awful quick for anyone that's new in a high position when they start in giving people under 'em the high hat."

"You saw Stella——"

"Well, I just noticed it as we came by you to shake hands at the reception, and it certainly didn't amount to much," Mr. Hedge returned. "I expect Stella was probably cordial enough to most of the crowd, but she certainly did hand it to Miss Nelson a little rough, Bill. Passed right over her, so to speak, and acted like she didn't know there was any such person as Miss Crystal Nelson. Kind of couldn't seem to see her at all, I thought, when Miss Nelson was offering to shake hands. Of course, as I say, it didn't amount to anything, and naturally there wasn't anything personal about it I don't suppose."

"No," William said seriously. "There couldn't have been because Stella never met Miss Nelson before. I'm afraid it was maybe just what you say, Henry—a touch of high hat. It won't do for Stella to give anybody a chance to think we're getting that way. I guess I better warn her about it."

"Maybe you might," Mr. Hedge agreed. "I'm not sure I ought to've mentioned it because it really didn't amount to anything at all; but women are mighty funny, Bill, mighty funny! You never can tell just what way anything's going to hit 'em, or which way they'll go. Stella's all right and she'll be just splendid in this new position if you give her just a little bit of guidance now and then, Bill; and she'll take it all right, too. She isn't like Aurelia." He sighed gently. "Aurelia, now, is kind of more headstrong."

"Yes," William said. "But Aurelia's a mighty fine woman, too, Henry."

Mr. Hedge sighed again. "Yes, she certainly is; she certainly is, Bill." Then he chuckled faintly. "I expect she and Stella are having a terrible grand powwow upstairs, Bill. Women always have to talk and talk and talk over and over and over anything like the big doings to-night. It'd be funny if we could hear what they're saying. Probably we couldn't understand half of it."

"Probably we couldn't," William said, amused. "I expect we'd laugh if we could hear 'em!" Then, noticing that his friend yawned slightly, "I expect you'd like to get a chance to go to bed, Henry. Maybe you'd better call Aurelia on the telephone and ask her if Stella——"

"No," said Mr. Hedge. "I was thinking probably we're all kind of tired and you'd like to get to bed, yourself. Maybe you better call up our number and ask Stella if she isn't coming down."

"All right," William returned; but he did not move and remained for a few moments in thought; then he said: "I expect she's pretty excited and having a good time talking it over. I don't like to interrupt her; but maybe it'd be a good thing if you'd call up Aurelia—she must be pretty tired, too—and ask her if Stella isn't coming down pretty soon."

Mr. Hedge looked uncertain; but he acquiesced, went to the telephone and presently called into it the number of his apartment. The voice of Aurelia responded to his ear:

"What do you want?"

"Look here, Aurelia," he said. "I was just thinking Bill's been through a good deal to-night and he looks kind of tired. He can't go to bed as long as I'm here and I haven't got any place else to go, so if you and Stella are maybe about through talking, why I thought perhaps——"

The voice of Aurelia in his ear responded fiercely, "Oh, shut up!"

He set the instrument meekly down upon the table, sighed, returned to his chair, and again elevated his feet upon the gilt radiator. "I guess not," he murmured. "Seems like they probably want to talk a little more, Bill."

Bill assented; and, for a time, they sat in silence, smoking desultorily. Then they fell into talk concerning the N.K.U., Promotion Marks and business prospects. An hour passed before they heard a light step in the corridor; the door was flung open and the bright presence of Stella seemed to fill the room with color and a sharp illumination.

VII

M Y GOOD heavens!" she cried, and her voice was high pitched with an excitement not lessened in this aftermath of her glorious evening, but heightened. "Haven't you two men any sense at all? Don't you ever know when it's time to go to bed?"

Henry Hedge laughed dryly, took his coat from the chair, folded it over his arm and, with no other response to Stella's sally than to bid her and William goodnight, departed and left the Greeleys alone together.

With the closing of the door William took a step toward his wife, and there was a movement of his arms that denoted an impulse to enfold her in a mutually congratulatory embrace. He was tired, somewhat enervated by the great evening, especially by the emotions incident to his oratorical effort, and what he wanted was to express a little affectionate satisfaction, to hear something of the same kind from Stella and then as soon as possible to get what he was thinking of as "some good old sound sleep." Smilingly, he half yawned as he took the step toward her. "Well, old lady," he began, "we've certainly had a grand——"

But Stella turned quickly to her dressing table and sat down before the mirror with her back toward him. "I wish he wouldn't smell up this apartment with his cheap cigars," she said, and, leaning closer to the glass, unclasped the necklace of crystal beads her husband had given her upon the fifth anniversary of their wedding. She dangled them between her eyes and the light above her mirror, then held them against her gold hair, like a wreath or slender coronet made of glittering little drops of ice; she gazed intently at this effect in the glass as she spoke. "I do wish if he's got to smoke in here he'd buy better cigars."

"Old Henry?" Her husband, a little disappointed, turned aside and, having already begun his undressing, hung up his coat and waistcoat in a shallow closet in the wall. Then he sat down to remove his shoes. "Poor old cuss, I was just thinking that we'll miss him—and Aurelia too, of course—when we move away from here. Henry was a mighty good friend to us when we first came to this town, and we four have always got along mighty well together. Of course we'll see a lot of 'em and all that, but naturally things aren't going to be quite the same as they have been here."

"Won't they? You think they won't?" his wife inquired, and, putting the crystal beads down upon the table, she slowly unfastened one of the earrings that matched them. "I expect we'll see just about as much of them as ever."

"Oh, yes, of course," he assented. "But it won't be the same as running in and out of each other's apartments the way you and Aurelia do here—not with us living in a house over a mile away."

"Won't it?" Stella uttered the short laugh of superior knowledge. "There are other houses in that neighborhood."

"What?"

"Certainly," Stella said. "Aurelia's absolutely decided it. They're going to rent a house near ours, and she and I are going up there to look for one right away. It's all set, and she's going to tell Henry about it to-night."

"Why, he can't afford it. They can't do it—especially not in that neighborhood. Henry's salary couldn't possibly stand it."

"Couldn't it?" Stella laughed again in the same superior manner. "Perhaps the salary he's getting now couldn't, but he may have a higher one before long, you see. I think there won't be much difficulty about fixing up a raise for Henry."

William shook his head ruefully. "Stella, there isn't any chance of it. Good old Henry's fixed just where he is for the rest of his days; he knows it, himself, and he likes it."

"Aurelia doesn't," Stella said. "Do you suppose she likes living here in this terrible old beehive? She almost cried when we were talking about it to-night before we decided what to do. This place is just about half full of small-town people that have only been in the city a few years, and Aurelia loathes 'em."

William was carrying his patent-leather shoes to the closet. "'Small-town people that have only been in the city a few years'!" he repeated. He dropped the shoes upon the floor of the closet and turned toward Stella. "My goodness! Why, that's what we are, ourselves! It's what Aurelia and Henry are, too, isn't it?"

"No," Stella answered quickly. "Maybe it's what we used to be, but not any more. If there's one thing in the world I hate it's this small-town gabble you hear all over the place from these new N.K.U. people especially, and Aurelia hates it worse than I do. If

there's one thing on earth that makes her go just
raving crazy, she always says, it's anything that's
jay. She says that what Mr. Cooper was talking
about to-night in his speech means that now there's
going to be more of that than ever—people from the
chain of hardware stores getting promotions and
coming up to the city. They're just the kind to move
in here, and she says she absolutely cannot stand it;
they're just as small-town after they get here as they
were in their own awful little county seats. What she
says is true, too. She was talking about what a
miserable, cheap, one-horse greenhorn life we all led
in Bennettsville before we got a chance to get out of
it. Well, we thought the Warwicke Armes was grand
when we moved in here, but now we know that it's
just about half full of Bennettsville kind of people,
and it makes Aurelia sick to think of staying here.
You might just as well know it once for all, Bill: I
intend to keep Aurelia near me and I'm going to see
that she has a house as close to ours as we can find
one."

He was perturbed and stared at her, frowning.
"Why, of course I'd be as glad as anybody," he
said, "if I could see any possible hope of Henry's
salary getting raised so he could afford it. I'd cer-

tainly do anything I could, but there isn't any way
to——"

"Isn't there?" Stella smiled surreptitiously to the
mirror and gave her lovely head a little toss. "I
think it can be managed."

"You do? I wish *I* did! I'd give a good deal to see
how I could——"

"You?" Stella interrupted coolly. "Oh, no; you
couldn't do anything."

"You see, Stella, the way Cooper and his father
before him built up the N.K.U., the factory manager
stands right next to the Big Boss; but in spite of that
the manager's never been allowed to have much
to do with the upper department promotions. I
couldn't——"

She swung about suddenly in her chair to face
him and, to his utter astonishment, the expression
upon her beautiful face seemed to be one of cold
hostility. "Who's talking about you? Nobody's asked
you to do anything, have they?"

"Why, Stella——"

But again, with her little laugh superiorly knowing,
she cut him short. "Never mind! I expect if I got
you where you are I could prob'ly do a little thing
like this!"

Her husband, dazed, stared at her hard. "If you got me where I am," he muttered. "You got me——"

"Good gracious!" she cried sharply. "Do you think I don't count for anything? You act like you thought I was nothing at all and you were everything."

"Well, but Stella, look here!"

"Yes, you do!" she cried. "You behave like you thought I was just a mere nothing except to pick up your collars and clean up your apartment after your friends have left ashes from their cheap cigars all over the floor, and do a hired girl's work for you, and never be anything of the slightest importance myself. That's the way you've always behaved to me from the very first day we were married, and I guess it's about time for you to understand that I'm getting tired of it!"

The good William was greatly troubled. He came to her and tried to put his hand on her shoulder. "My gracious me, Stella!" he said. "You've been on a strain, and you're all tired out. It's been too much for you and you're getting hysterical."

This effort to soothe was apparently misplaced. She drew back from his hand and jumped up. "Don't touch me! I'd think you'd be man enough to understand that after the fine speech you made to-night

I wouldn't be caring to have you trying to paw me!"

"Oh, golly!" he moaned. "You weren't any more ashamed of me for that speech than I was of myself, Stella; I expect you're right; it certainly was a terrible thing. I don't blame you."

"Yes, it was terrible," she agreed angrily. "But you don't know yet half how terrible it was."

"Oh my! Oh my! Yes, I do. Nobody could think it was awfuller than I do, Stella. You couldn't possibly think any worse——"

"Oh, yes, I could," she said, and laughed bitterly. "You haven't got gumption enough to see what you did and how it made you look. Honestly, I should think you'd rather have died than get up there before all those people and do what you did to me!"

At this he was sure of her hysteria. "Now, for heaven's sake, let's go to bed and get some rest. I don't believe you know a word you're saying: it actually sounds like you're out of your head."

"You think so!"

"Why, yes—talking about what I did to you——"

"You don't see it yet? When Mr. Cooper and every one of those men said what they did, and then you got up and said what you did! Did you hear what those other men said?"

"Well, I suppose I did—in a way. I was so flustered trying to remember what I was going to say, myself, and worrying about it and perspiring and all——"

"Oh, you heard them!" she interrupted sharply. "Don't pretend to me that you didn't hear them simply because they praised your wife."

"What?" he gasped. "What in the world——"

"Yes, you did! You heard every word. You heard Mr. Cooper, himself, say how responsible I was for your success and how you'd never in the world have amounted to anything if it hadn't been for me! You heard them all, one after the other; you saw them stand up there and say what they did about me—and then you get up and make an exhibition of yourself that's just pitiable, and I guess everybody in that whole place wondered why, if all those other men thought I deserved the appreciation and praise they gave me, my own husband didn't even utter a single word about me. That was a nice thing for me to endure, wasn't it? When all the others——"

"Oh, my goodness!" William moaned. "I just never thought of it. I wrote out that terrible speech of mine in the office and tried to learn it by heart, and kept practising it whenever I was alone all afternoon. After I got on my feet, I couldn't have changed it, or said anything different, even if it had occurred to me that it would be proper to put in a compliment to you, or something."

"And of course it never occurred to you to put one in while you were writing your speech! It never occurred to you that you owed me anything for getting you where you are. It never occurred to you even when you heard what Mr. Cooper and those other men said about how you owed your success to——"

"Oh, for heaven's sake!" William, mystified and distressed, was becoming also a little nettled. "I tell you I couldn't have changed my speech, after I got started, to save my soul. Those other men all know how to speak, and they put in what they said about you just on the spur of the moment, as it were. They know how to do things like that and I don't, and I'm sorry I don't; I wish I did. But, see here, they said all that about you a good deal because you were looking your best to-night, Stella, and, for heaven's sake don't get to thinking they meant it seriously, and don't let it give you the big head, Stella. And that reminds me, there's something I wanted to talk to you about—I didn't mean to bring it up until to-morrow morning at breakfast; but I guess I might as well go ahead with it now."

"Go ahead with it," she said, breathing rapidly. "Go ahead with it."

"Well, it's just this," William began, somewhat doggedly. "It's just this, Stella: the way it looks to me, all that flattery and everything you heard to-night I thought was just fine while it was going on; and I'll admit I was kind of proud, myself, to hear them making such a fuss over you; but, good land! I didn't dream it was going to upset you and start you to thinking you've done all this and that, instead of my own work's doing it, and I certainly never dreamed it would start you to high-hatting people you ought to be mighty nice and friendly with. I certainly never dreamed any such a thing as that, Stella."

"Didn't you?" she asked. "Who did I high-hat?"

"Listen!" he said. "How did you treat Miss Nelson at the reception? What did you do when she came up to shake hands with you?" Then, as Stella gave a gasp of anger and started back from him, he lifted a hand of entreaty. "Now wait! I'm not saying it amounted to much, or that I meant to take you to task for it exactly; and anyhow it might have been partly accidental——"

"No, it wasn't," she interrupted. "Don't think for a minute that there was any accident about it. You have the nerve to stand there and ask me how I treated Miss Crystal Nelson! I treated her the way I'm always going to treat her, and if you don't like it you better look out!"

With that, she swung away from him and began to pull her dress off over her head. As for her husband, he dropped down upon a chair. "I don't know what's come over you," he said. "You've never been the same since the day after I landed the big job. I noticed the difference in you right away then, Stella; but I didn't say anything about it because I thought as soon as you got used to it you'd be more like yourself again. But every single minute you've acted flightier and flightier, until now I actually believe you've plumb lost your balance. What in the name of common sense have you got against Miss Crystal Nelson?"

From within the sack of cornflower colored chiffon in which her head and upper body was enveloped, the voice of Stella came viciously. "Oh, dry up!" Then, as she emerged and went to hang her dress in a closet opposite that wherein William had hung his coat and waistcoat, and deposited his shoes, she sent him a shrewish glance over her pretty shoulder. "Ask Mrs. Thomas! Ask Mrs. Peale!"

Upon this, William was completely blank. "Ask Mrs. Thomas and Mrs. Peale?"

Stella turned away from the closet. "I'll let you know right now that what happened to them isn't going to happen to me!" she said.

"What happened to Mrs. Thomas and Mrs. Peale? What did happen to 'em?"

"Miss Crystal Nelson happened to 'em," Stella answered grimly. "If you don't know what goes on under the surface in the N.K.U. it's about time you learned."

"You mean to say——"

"Listen!" she interrupted imperiously. "It's about time that young woman's activities ended. Mrs. Peale couldn't stand her husband having that girl for his secretary, and so she made him resign, then when Mrs. Thomas couldn't stand the same thing any longer Mr. Thomas had to resign. That isn't going to happen to me."

William rubbed his forehead. "My land! Do you have to believe every piece of crazy gossip you hear? Peale had to quit because the Big Boss decided he was losing his efficiency, and so did Thomas."

"Is that so?" Stella returned scornfully. "Perhaps you didn't know they were both retired at their own request because their wives made them."

"That's pure nonsense. Everybody high up in the N.K.U. 'retires at his own request.' That's just a form when a tip from the Big Boss gets into the air that there's going to be retirements. I'd be 'retired at my own request,' myself, if I began to get wind of such a tip."

Quickly and surprisingly, upon this, Stella uttered a loud and shrill laugh. "Yes, I guess you would! Maybe you better look out you're not retired at somebody else's request."

"Somebody else's? Why, whose?"

"At mine!" She came toward him furiously. "Oh, you needn't sit there and goggle at me because I tell you, right here and now, something like that's liable to happen if you don't watch your step mighty carefully. Let me tell you I guess I know quite a few things about your Miss Nelson!"

"She isn't my Miss Nelson, and just for instance, what do you know about her?"

"I know one thing: you're not going to sit there day after day dictating to her!"

"You're right about that, Stella," he returned

promptly. "But it looks to me as if you were mistaken in thinking you know so much about her. I don't dictate letters to Miss Nelson; there's a stenographer for that. I don't think you understand. I'm supposed to run the N.K.U. plants. My secretary looks after all the office details, and let me tell you that's a pretty important job because it includes the Big Boss's office details, too—his own secretary is the kind you're thinking about; just takes dictation and runs errands. Miss Nelson's been with the N.K.U. a good part of her life; she knows it like a book, and, while she's mighty quiet and never puts on anything to be important, she's always there with the goods. What's more, I said a while ago that I'm holding down a job that puts me right next to the Big Boss himself; but I'm not so plumb sure about that as I might be, and for just this reason: Cooper only spends about two hours a day at the offices, and about all he ever says to Miss Nelson when he comes in is just 'Good morning.' But the longer I've been with the N.K.U. the more I've sort of thought she had a good deal of influence with him. What I mean, if there is anybody that's more next to him than the factory manager, why it's the factory manager's secretary. That's why

I think that if you had to begin high-hatting people, Stella, you began at the wrong place."

"Oh, I did, did I?" Stella was angrier than ever, and again she laughed shrilly. "Because your Miss Nelson has so much influence with Mr. Cooper and not because she's already got so much with you? Oh, no! You aren't concerned about her at all, and yet, by your own confession, all he ever says to her is just 'good morning'!" Stella's laughter became louder and shriller. "I never heard anything like it in my life! You're not very hard to see through, Bill Greeley. Do you suppose I don't see what you're fixing to tell me?"

"I'm not fixing to tell you anything," he returned, irritated. "I don't know what you're talking about. What am I fixing to tell you?"

"You're going to try and put it over on me that if you tried to fire her Mr. Cooper would interfere and wouldn't let you; that's exactly what you're trying to do."

"I am not, and I'm not thinking of firing her either."

"But if you were," Stella said mockingly. "If you were, Mr. Cooper wouldn't let you, would he?"

"I don't know whether he would or not; I kind of think he wouldn't; but what's that got to do with it? I'm not thinking of firing her."

"Why aren't you thinking of it?" she demanded.

He jumped up, facing her. "Because there isn't any reason on earth why I should do such a thing."

"No? Not if your wife demands it?"

William, goaded, was becoming desperate. "Stella, you're acting like a crazy woman! What on earth's Miss Nelson ever done to you? She's never done anything at all except attend to her own business, and I've always had the highest admiration for her on account of the way she does attend to it. Then just the little time since I've been factory manager and had her working with me has made me see I could hardly run the place without her, though I could pretty nearly believe she could run it without me. I'd no more think of handing her out her walking papers than I'd——"

"What about your own?" And now there glistened a sudden water of anger along Stella's eyelids. "What about your own walking papers? You don't think you're in any danger of my handing you out yours when you dare to talk to me like that!"

"What?" he gasped.

"I mean it!" she cried. "After your talking to me like this, that woman either goes or I won't live with you. You dare to stand up here and defend her and praise her to my very face? You call your wife a crazy woman and in the same breath you gush and mush all over *her*—you call your wife a lunatic and then go ranting around about how you been admiring Crystal Nelson for years and years! You can get along without your wife, all right, but you can't get along without Crystal Nelson. Your wife ought to be put in an asylum, but Crystal Nelson is a goddess that runs the whole N.K.U.! Crazy am I? Let me tell you, William Greeley, I'm not as crazy as you are if you expect me to sit and bear a thing like this and not do anything about it. Either I get rid of that woman, or I leave you!"

Her unfortunate husband was at the end of his resources. "Well, either you're crazy or I am. You're certainly behaving like a crazy——"

Stella screamed aloud. "Crazy! You call me that again, do you? I'll show you which one of us is crazy. You may find out that you and that woman aren't running the whole N.K.U.! Crazy am I? I'll show you who——"

"Stella! Stella!" he begged piteously. "You'll

have everybody in all the apartments around here hammering on our door to see what's the matter. For mercy's sake, stop your noise!"

Stella threw herself full length upon the maroon velvet sofa, and wept aloud. "I'll show you!" she sobbed. "That woman's a goddess and your wife's a lunatic! You'll find out! Yes, and she'll find out, too! She'll find out how much of a goddess the N.K.U. thinks she is when I have her put out of there. You stand up before a thousand people and can't say a decent word about your wife; and then you come home and call me a lunatic. You'll see whether I bear it or not! You'll see! You'll see! You'll see!"

William opened the mirror-faced doors that concealed the bed, which was already made up for the night; he pulled the bed down and sat upon it, groaning, "Oh, dearie me, dearie me, dearie me! Everything was all right between us until I got this big job. I wish to heaven the N.K.U. had let me alone where I was. I'd never have taken it if I'd thought it was going to do anything like this to us. I don't understand it; honestly, I don't. I don't understand how on earth such a trouble as this could have happened to us, Stella."

His wife continued to sob into one of the two

maroon colored velvet sofa pillows, and he remained sitting upon the bed, muttering woefully to himself at intervals. Never in his life had he known greater distress, or puzzlement so acute; and in this latter phase, his emotional bewilderment, he had not much the advantage, if he had known it, of his wife. For Stella, suffering although she was from the jealousy she had built up within herself, did not know why she had built it, and, beneath all the tumultuous surface of her agitation, she felt almost as profound a puzzlement as William did himself.

VIII

THIS puzzlement of Stella's was so far down within her that her consciousness of it was vague; it was so far down and so vague, indeed, that it needed a special stimulus to bring it upon the surface of her feeling. Such a stimulus, however, did make her almost definitely aware of that obscure bewilderment of hers on the following morning when, after an almost silent breakfast, William had departed and Columbine Watson had arrived. Columbine Watson was a young colored woman engaged to do the housework of the apartment in the mornings; Stella had thus indulged herself for the interval preceding removal to the new house. She had felt that not only would Columbine be a present convenience, but that in the direction of this servitress there might be useful practice in an unfamiliar art, knowledge of which the management of a house would soon demand of her. Her reproach to William that he made use of her to clean up the ashes of his friends' cheap cigars, therefore, might have appeared ill-founded, for it was Columbine who brushed into a dustpan what Mr. Hedge had thoughtlessly left upon the floor near the radiator; nevertheless, it was while the colored woman was so engaged that Stella again made the same complaint.

"I was too tired last night to sweep that up, myself, Columbine," she said, and she went on, with a rueful little laugh, "I've swept up a good many piles of ashes for my husband and his friends in my time, though. I expect if all the ashes I've swept up for him could be gathered into one heap it'd make a mountain."

Columbine laughed sympathetically. "Yes'm. Yes'm, I expeck so. You hadn't of ought to been sweepin' up no ashes, Miz Greeley. You got too pretty hands fer sweepin' up ole dirty cigar ashes."

Stella, at her dressing table, looked first at her hands and then at their reflection in the mirror. "Have I? These hands of mine have done a pretty good deal of hard work for my husband, Columbine." She sighed deeply. "Well, I've never complained; I've just gone ahead the best I knew how." Then she laughed sadly again. "Much it's been appreciated!"

Columbine was instantly prepared to agree with

her. "No'm, I expeck not. Look to me like mos' ladies gits mighty little 'preciation from the dear ones they loves bes'." She carried the ashes to a tin bucket, emptied them there, and began to wipe the wooden parts of the furniture with a rag. "Las' month I was helpin' house-clean fer Miz T. S. Williams on Bellefontaine Boulevard. Her husban' jes' the same way, she tell me, Miz Greeley. Miz T. S. Williams say many's the time she jes' set and cry, her husban' behave' so mean. 'Way I look at it, it's in 'em, Miz Greeley. Yes'm, they jes' got it in 'em. I ain't hardly worked fer more'n jes about two ladies in all my life that had husban's they had a real good word to say fer. 'Way I look at it, Miz Greeley, a husban' is a husban', and nothin' in the worl' ain't goin' to git that out of him. If a man ain't your husban', seems like he knows how to behave mighty nice; but the minute he gets to be your husban', why, he begin that very minute to be one. I tell you frankly, Miz Greeley, that's my own experience, and I thank the good heaven above us I've seen the kindly light never to git married no more. Anybody else want a husban', go on and take him; I see my salvation without any. It's a shame Mr. Greeley ain't talk nicer to you, Miz Greeley. You only got to look in that lookin'-glass to see why he ought to go down on his knees and give thanks every minute he's got such a wife!"

"I guess you're right about husbands, Columbine," Stella said. "They aren't very likely to be going down on their knees and giving thanks for anything like that. I expect mine would prob'ly be more apt to go down on his knees and give thanks if he could get rid of me."

Columbine uttered a little cry of sympathy and protest. "Miz Greeley! Why, I couldn' hardly believe what you tell me. How come Mr. Greeley use you so mean? What he been doin'?" Her eyes sparkled with interest. "He ain't never hit you, is he, Miz Greeley?"

"No," Stella said slowly, "he hasn't." And, to her own surprise, she added, "Not yet."

"Did he make like he was goin' to hit you, Miz Greeley?"

"No," Stella said, "it's not that I'm afraid of, but there are things a wife can suffer that are worse than being struck."

"Yes'm; indeed they can, indeed they can! My firs' husban' jes' like that, Miz Greeley. Tuck and call me names till I simply had to resist him; and he even brought false testimony agains' me in court on account of it. But I reckon Mr. Greeley ain't called you no names like what my firs' husban' called me, Miz Greeley."

"I don't know. I don't know," Stella said. "Did your first husband call you a crazy woman and a lunatic!"

"Miz Greeley! You don' mean to set there and tell me Mr. Greeley use' you like that?"

"Don't I?" Stella said; and, stirred by her recollection of this grievance, suddenly she sniffled.

"Miz Greeley! I declare my heart bleed' fer you; I declare it do. If you hadn't set there and tole me yourself I wouldn' never a-b'lieve' any man blessed enough to be your lifeways companion would let his wicked tongue belabor itself towards you, like you tell me."

"No," Stella said desolately, "I don't suppose anyone would believe it unless they heard it. People see a woman going around wearing a smile, doing her best to always look cheerful, and they don't think what she may have to be bearing at home; they don't know what she goes through when she's alone with her husband, and what she has to stand from him." She sighed painfully, and wiped her eyes with a little handkerchief from her dressing table. "Well, I guess there's only one thing to do and that is to bear it."

Her tone was pathetic, and even as she spoke she, herself, realized that it was intentionally so. Moreover, her realization that she was almost deliberately trying to evoke for herself the sympathy of this lowly but willing comrade in grief was what brought up to the surface of her feeling the puzzlement that lay so deep within her. Suddenly, this puzzlement became acute: how had it come about that she was talking like this, trying to make her husband odious to even a chance passer-by in their lives like this colored woman? Why had she been impelled to attack him last night, and why did she feel the impulse now to complain of him and to injure him? In the last depths of her heart that were left pellucid she did not believe that as a wife she stood in any danger from Miss Nelson. It was not jealousy she felt but a kind of imitation of jealousy; as if such a mimicry of that passion had been a necessity, and she perceived, though only vaguely, that she had grasped at the imitation. After her glorious evening she had come down from Aurelia's room elated, triumphant, her imagination more than ever vibrant with the ballet spectacle in which she engaged in a dance of the utmost romantic possibility with the kingly and infatuated figure of Mr. Milton Cooper. Then, away from Aurelia's hilariously admiring and planful presence, and alone with William, she had felt that jealous anger with him, or that imitation of jealous anger, rising and rising; and now, as she talked to Columbine, she felt it still rising, even though somewhere within her a little of her knew that it was spurious. Nevertheless, she was acting upon its promptings, and knew that she would continue so to act.

Nor in this prognostication was she mistaken. The outspoken sympathy of even Mrs. Columbine Watson had its effect: hearing herself pitied by another, Stella pitied herself the more; her puzzlement withdrew from the surface and was accompanied out of sight by that curious sense of her jealousy's spuriousness, and she was again able, almost with conviction, to believe herself an ill-used woman. Going forth with Aurelia in the latter's sedan, she gave her friend a plaintive account of William's insulting words, but without mentioning anything that had provoked them.

Aurelia, however, was of a practical mind. "Had you been telling him you wouldn't stand for Miss Nelson?"

"Yes, I had. I told him either she'd go or I would!"

"Murder!" Aurelia laughed gayly. "What do you care?"

"What?"

"What do you care?" Aurelia repeated merrily. "The more he and Crystal Nelson get talked about, the better it'll be for everything else, the way I look at it. I haven't heard how much worse Mrs. Cooper's flu is; but suppose things did turn out so that it would be the best thing for you to get a cute little divorce pretty soon, why, don't you see, if everybody's talking about Bill and Miss Nelson——"

"Can't you ever quit that?" Stella cried, and laughed excitedly. "You certainly are the worst cut-up!"

Aurelia was delighted. "We don't know where we're going," she sang, "but we're on our way!" Then her air became one of sympathetic concern. "All the same, I think Bill ought to be ashamed of himself for bawling you out the way he did last night. It was simply outrageous, and I think he ought to be made to feel it. I wouldn't blame you for telling the whole N.K.U. all about it."

Thus prompted, Stella again, and yet more keenly, felt the sting of her wrongs; she did not intend to tell the whole N.K.U. about them, as Aurelia suggested; but, later in the day, she was unable to resist an impulse to get a little sympathy from Mrs. Caples. The three ladies sat, supplied with "sundaes" and cakes, at a table in a confectioner's shop, and Mrs. Caples had just finished some warmly congratulatory remarks upon Stella's appearance at the banquet. Then she became a little arch.

"It was almost like being at a play in a theatre," she said gayly. "For my part I didn't need to hear what Mrs. Hedge told us about the orchids and all to see which way the wind was blowing. Every time Mr. Cooper looked at you—well, I guess we better not go into that! You certainly adorned your position, Mrs. Greeley. I'm sure you must be a very happy woman."

Stella murmured "Thank you" in a low voice, and looked away.

Mrs. Caples was surprised. "You don't mean to say you aren't the happiest woman in the world?"

"Happiest?" Stella murmured. "I suppose I should be; but I'm afraid I'm not. No, Mrs. Caples, I'm afraid I'm not very happy to-day."

"Oh!" Mrs. Caples, instantly eager, tried to look as though she had no wish to intrude upon a private matter. "I'm terribly sorry," she said, and sought the eye of Aurelia who shook her head in unspoken lament, sighed and then obligingly breathed, in the slightest of whispers, the words "It's her husband."

"Oh, dear me," Mrs. Caples said. "I am so sorry to hear it." She leaned toward Stella with a manner of benevolent compassion that formed an excellent surface over a perfectly natural inward self-congratulation upon the fact that this chance encounter at the confectioner's was becoming so interesting. "My dear child," she said, "I think I'm enough older than you to remind you that you're still comparatively very young, and that young married people always have their troubles. You mustn't take things too seriously. Remember that your husband is young, too, and he's lately been elevated to a position that might turn any man's head. At his age to be put up above a great many older men who've been much longer in the N.K.U. than he has couldn't very well be without its effect upon him. We wives must remember that men are very queer creatures, my dear, and that especially in moments of triumph they're apt to forget and neglect us, and even to seem a little impatient with us. Most of all they're apt to forget the share we've had in their success."

A beautiful tear appeared upon Stella's left cheek.

"That's not all they forget," she said in a broken whisper.

"No, of course not," Mrs. Caples agreed quickly. "But, my dear, I think we must always remember to make allowances. They may wander a little from the fold, but they always come back, my dear; they always come back."

"Maybe they don't if they get to wandering away with Miss Crystal Nelson," Aurelia blurted out, as if she could not help it. Immediately, she seized upon one of Stella's hands and gripped it in hot sympathy. "I know I shouldn't say it, but some things just make my blood boil and I can't help it. When, just because a man's got a swelled head about himself, he hasn't got sense enough to appreciate the woman who put him where he is, and talks to her like she was the mere dregs of the earth and——"

"Oh, no!" Mrs. Caples protested, horrified. "I could never believe such a thing! With a wife like Mrs. Greeley, I simply couldn't be convinced that anybody with no better looks than Miss Nelson——"

"All right," Aurelia interrupted briskly. "Just ask Stella what he said to her last night."

Stella made a murmur of protest, and, for a moment a sense of annoyance prevailed over the

pathos she had been feeling for herself; curiously
enough, she had a momentary impulse to set up some
sort of defense, however lame, for the offending
William. He was her husband, not Aurelia's; and
she felt that if he was to be defamed the defamation
was her own affair, not any other woman's. "Aurelia,
it isn't your business to be saying such things about
Mr. Greeley. Besides that, you'll make Mrs. Caples
think he's behaving worse to me than he is, and the
very last thing I want to do is to begin setting
people against him."

"Of course," Mrs. Caples said tenderly. "Of course
you feel that way, you poor dear thing!"

"Yes—I do." Stella's voice, under the influence of
this ready compassion, again became a little broken.
"I've spent my life working for him, and if he doesn't
appreciate it and shows he doesn't—like last
night——" She faltered.

"Oh, my!" Mrs. Caples exclaimed. "Last night, of
all nights! Just when every one of those distinguished
men and Mr. Cooper, himself, had been saying how
wonderful you were, and all!" Her tone became
indignant. "I can't believe it! Really, I can hardly
believe that any sane man would be so wicked as to
come home after hearing such tributes to his wife

and say cruel and unkind things to her. I can't believe it. If Mr. Greeley did such a thing he simply must have been crazy."

"Oh, no," Stella said wanly. "That's what he thought I was."

"What!"

"Oh, yes," Stella said. "'Lunatic' was among the other things he called me."

"Oh, dear, dear, dear!" Mrs. Caples moaned. "And that was the end of your evening of triumph. I never knew anything so heartbreaking. I'm afraid that is bad, my dear; yes, I'm afraid that's pretty bad!"

IX

STELLA, herself, had just begun to feel that it was indeed pretty bad, though not in the sense intended by Mrs. Caples; her puzzlement had unexpectedly returned to the surface, and she sat wondering how on earth it had come about that she was again doing what she could to injure her husband. Until a few weeks ago, she had never in her life either spoken or hinted ill of him; on the contrary, she had often bragged of him, and had ever been his ready and affectionate champion. Even now, in spite of all she did and said, her affection for him still existed; and yet it seemed that to speak ill of him was on the point of becoming her habit. Suddenly such a habit appeared to her as a horrible one; and for an instant there shot within her bosom a strange, breathless fear that she, herself, was horrible. This small and icy fright of hers passed rapidly; and indeed the unfortunate lady need not have felt it, for she had no cause to fear that she was horrible, or that what she was doing held any horribleness. What she did was not horrible; it was natural, and she, herself, was not exceptional; she was merely the servant of natural human impulse. Her puzzlement was that of a wife whose flights of fancy have sought the air about an alluring figure not her husband's; for, since a wife must feel that such a flying of fancies is a threatened blow to the husband, she must instinctively seek to possess herself of resentment against him, because our natures so order us that if we are to strike we must, if we can, be spurred to the blow by resentment. Stella was gropingly trying to acquire the resentment that would be necessary if destiny should solidify castles in the air; for compunction of any kind never finds place in such castles so long as they remain in the air, where hers at this juncture still obviously were. She did not understand that her own nature and the nature of her gilding new fancy required her to manufacture within her as much feeling against William (no matter how little he, himself, incited) as she possibly could. No more than she, did Aurelia comprehend such simple laws of our being, although this accommodating Aurelia instinctively furnished her friend with all the needed resentment she could supply; nor was Aurelia horrible, either.

The brisk Aurelia, indeed, had no suspicion of

any horribleness anywhere, and she lived now for the new excitement of every fresh hour. Her early jealousy of Stella's rise had long since disappeared entirely; but, although she meant to take benefit of that rise herself, her great pleasure, now, was that of the intimate subordinate who dresses the belle for the ball. Aurelia was even unaware that the dress for the belle was made of goose feathers supplied by herself; she forgot that she had made it. Cooking out of cans for the melancholy and resigned Henry took too little of Aurelia's time; and, having no fertile place in her head for anything not personal and of the moment, nor any affairs of her own that were not of a dull routine, she had either to be busy with her neighbors and their affairs, continually finding new sensations for herself therein, or to perish of ennui. Thus, the more sensational Stella's affair became, the more happily did Aurelia hold at bay the vacuum ever ready to occupy her own head; naturally, therefore, she built up the romance as energetically as she could.

"Bad," she said, repeating this word of Mrs. Caples's and making it ominously eloquent. "I'm afraid if you knew everything you'd say it's worse than bad."

Stella checked her. "Never mind!" But the ardent friend was not so easily to be suppressed.

A waitress came with the account, and, as Stella opened her purse and found the money to pay it, Aurelia leaned closer to Mrs. Caples, whispering indignantly, "To think that with a man worth millions ready to marry her any minute he's free, a woman should have to put up with such outrages from a spoiled little snip of a husband that thinks he's Napoleon just because he's been stuck up over *our* heads in the N.K.U. and——"

This whisper was left unfinished; but no doubt it had its effect, for Mrs. Caples, as her many acquaintances knew by instructive experience, was a sort of town crier or walking news sheet for the circulation of all matters public and private, rumor or fact, pertaining to the N.K.U. Her distribution of what she had been filled with in the confectioner's shop must have been both rapid and thorough, for not many days passed before it brought some discomfiture upon William Greeley, himself. This troubled gentleman already had enough of perplexity to burden a heretofore equable and kindly disposition, it may be said; his domestic life, within the short space of time elapsed since his promotion, had become unbearable;

and he was completely mystified to find it so. Naturally he was not at a loss to attribute his unhappiness to the alteration in Stella; but the only explanation of the difference in her seemed to be that suddenly improved prospects in life had gone destructively to her head. The explanation appeared to be doubtful but there could be no question of the destruction, for his peace of mind and hers, too, were obviously in a state of ruin.

After their bitter quarrel, which more and more astonishingly seemed to him a senseless and inexplicable one, he waited a day, then approached her with apologetic hints of affection, and made overtures for a truce of reasonableness. "To save my life, dearie," he said, "I can't think what it is that's come between us. Maybe I'm in fault; I don't know. And, if I am, I certainly am sorry for it. It'd be terrible for us to go on like this—not saying a thing to each other unless we're just forced to, and shut up here in the same room, the way we are, until the house is ready for us to move into it. Besides, if I go down to the N.K.U. thinking about this trouble, when I ought to be thinking about my work, the way I did to-day, why, it's going to get me rattled; it scares me about not making good, and it's dangerous for a man in my position to be scared of that. He's got to be sure he *is* making good, you see, Stella. So, let's just try and sit down together, and see if we can't find out what's wrong between us. Won't you, for both our sakes, dearie?"

"Both whose sakes?" she inquired and she laughed contemptuously. "Yours and Miss Crystal Nelson's?"

"Oh, my glory! You're at that again, are you? I don't suppose I've exchanged words with Miss Nelson a dozen times this whole day. Honestly, I think you must be——" He paused abruptly, but she finished the sentence for him.

"Crazy?" she inquired calmly. "Going to call me a lunatic again, weren't you?"

He offered amends. "Honestly, I don't mean to say such things to you, Stella; but the truth is you've got me rattled——"

"*I* have? *I!*"

He wiped his forehead. "I wasn't accusing you of anything, Stella. Seems as if I can't say a word that you don't take it like something against you. Why can't we get together the way we used to be? Looking back, it seems to me that we were always pretty happy, and certainly we never had any trouble like this before; if we could just sit down together and get at it, so to speak, why, probably we'd be all right again. Don't you want to try to do that, Stella?"

"You mean to give you the chance to call me a lunatic again?" she returned. "You make me tired."

He got no further with her then, nor upon his next attempt to reason with her did he get so far; she repulsed him fiercely at once, and he found himself wholly baffled.

"I don't know what's come over you. I guess I'll just have to give it up," he said sadly. "It looks to me as if you felt you had to keep yourself just deliberately set against me—as if you were just bound to keep on being furious with me, Stella, no matter what I say or what I do."

This was a gloomy and aimless shot from the dark, but unfortunately, as it struck the bull's-eye, it scored. It was a truth that Stella could acknowledge last of all to herself, a fact not possibly to be endured; her only way to face it was to take it as the most slanderous of all his insults, and she was never more furious with him. She went immediately to extremes: "You—you coward!" she cried; and then, with a volubility new to his experience of her, she began an arraignment, the end of which he did not remain to hear. He went forth and walked the streets until an hour when he could be sure that she had retired and gone to sleep; then came home, tired and bemused, and slept upon the maroon colored sofa.

His wife was not the only lady whose manner showed signs of change toward him. The expression of Mrs. Hedge, whom he saw most frequently, bothered him a little when she looked at him. Her eyes were arch and rallying, but they had a secret in them, a triumphant amusement that could not be shared with him, though he had a bewildered perception that it was shared with Stella. William and the mournful Henry were not unaccustomed to be excluded, temporarily at least, from secret understandings between the two ladies, and this one added no more than slightly to the new factory manager's disturbance of mind; what did increase that disturbance mightily, however, was some confidential advice offered to him by a woman not of the intimate and rather small N.K.U. and Warwicke Armes circle to which the Greeleys and Hedges had heretofore belonged. Some of William's former departmental colleagues had prepared a little celebration in honor of the Greeleys, a modest Saturday night supper in the Olde Englysshe Grill Room of the Warwicke

Armes, and it happened that Mrs. Gliesinger was seated next to William upon his left. She had been the "war bride" of one of the N.K.U. engineers, and, an Alsatian of homely and simple extraction, had not acquired the habit of resisting a benevolent impulse, or of regarding any subject whatever as embarrassing. The little banquet was noisy and hilarious; Mrs. Gliesinger easily made her conversation private to her neighbor's ear.

"I think you are such a fine man, Mr. Greeley. My husband say you are the finest man he thinks he know. He say you are the best man Mr. Cooper is ever going to find in this whole grand business. My husband say to me, 'Listen,' he say, 'Listen, and don't let anybody get you to believe all such things about Mr. Greeley. Mr. Greeley is too fine a man, so don't you believe it,' my husband tell me. Well, Mr. Greeley, I didn't know I would sit next to you to-night; but I am glad it happens because I would like to say to you, just you let them go on, Mr. Greeley, and pretty soon, if you are a little careful, they will be gabbling about something else."

William stared at her plaintively. "If I'm a little careful?" he said. "If I'm a little careful about what, Mrs. Gliesinger?"

"Ah, you don't need anyone to tell you," she returned, smiling. "But Gliesinger and I have been married longer than you and Mrs. Greeley, I think, so I will say a little something. First when we were married Gliesinger would go just crazy if he thinks I was giving some young man a smile out of the little edge of my eye. On the train once there were some boys coming home from their university—whee!" She laughed out heartily and clapped her hands together. "That Gliesinger! You would think he is going to throw me straight out through the window! People all must go through their married troubles, Mr. Greeley; but I could throw my arms around you now and that Gleisinger he would just laugh. Some day you must be like that too, Mr. Greeley; your wife is young and beautiful and not very busy, I think. It is natural that great attention would be made to her, and when great people make it perhaps it would put some ideas in her head; she might think a little foolish; then if you get jealous the way like my Gliesinger used to, and say all such rough things to her, she might be pushed too far. She might do more than think foolish; she might act foolish. Besides, when you get jealous and talk so angry to her, you help to make all this gabble that goes around. I would

just be a little careful, Mr. Greeley; be patient with
her, not jealous; then the gabble will stop."

"Gabble?" William repeated in a startled voice.
"Me jealous?"

Obviously altogether friendly, she nodded. "Yes;
of course when a man is as important as you are now,
Mr. Greeley, if he is jealous there has got to be a great
gabble."

"About my being jealous?" he gasped incredulously. "Upon my soul, Mrs. Gliesinger, I don't know
what you're talking about! I don't understand a word
of what you're telling me."

She beamed upon him and gave his arm a friendly
little pat. "Oh, yes," she said, "you understand me
very well, Mr. Greeley; but it is all right for you to
say you don't. It is what my Gliesinger would say if
someone would talk to him when we were first
married the way I have been talking to you. Anyhow
just be a little more careful and patient, Mr. Greeley.
Now we talk of something else, don't we?"

"But I don't understand," he insisted. "On my
word——"

He was interrupted; the party was drawing to a
close, and there was a loud demand that he and
Stella should rise to their feet and stand during a

chorus, "for Stella and Bill are jolly good fellows!"
The toast was heartily drunk in grapejuice mixed
with gingerale; the entire company then rose and,
with joined hands, sang "Auld Lang Syne"; and,
with this ceremony, the festivities ended. William
had no opportunity to press Mrs. Gliesinger for her
meaning.

X

BESET by a curiosity too painful to bear in silence, he determined to obtain light from Stella; but he knew he would have to wait until she came from the conference it was her nightly habit to hold with Aurelia in the latter's apartments before either couple could retire. Henry Hedge, with his bad cigar and flaccid with depression, was shunted off upon the perturbed factory manager for a full two hours of disjointed and spiritless conversation; but at last Stella appeared, and the Greeleys were left alone together.

"Look here," William said, after an interval of silence. "I'd made up my mind I wouldn't speak to you again about our trouble unless you spoke first; but I've got to break the rule. Have you been talking, Stella?"

"Certainly I've been talking," she returned airily. "I've been talking all evening to two nice men on each side of me and I'm about talked out. I don't care for any more to-night, thank you."

"I'm sorry but I expect you've got to listen to some, Stella."

"Have I? You mean I have to listen whether I want to or not?"

"Listen," he said sharply. "I want to know who's been filling Mrs. Gliesinger up with what she was telling me to-night."

"Mrs. Gliesinger? How do I know what Mrs. Gliesinger's filled up with? I scarcely go with her at all, and I don't know anything about her."

"It looks like that might be the point of it," he said. "If she hears such things, what have the people you do go with heard? And where'd they get hold of it? That's what I want to know."

"Why don't you ask them?"

"I'm asking you," he said slowly. "I'm asking you, Stella."

"Are you? That's right cute of you!" And Stella, who had begun her undressing at once upon her entrance into the room, whistled the air of "Auld Lang Syne" as she went on with rapid preparations for bed.

"I want an answer," he said heavily. "Mrs. Gliesinger had got it all wrong. The way the story reached her, I'm the one that's jealous."

Stella interrupted her whistling to laugh. "You are? Who of? Old Hank Hedge?"

"Somebody's been talking, Stella; and I want to know who it is. Somebody's started the story around that there's trouble between us and that I'm being tyrannical with you——"

"Well, what do you call this? I've told you that I'm tired to death, and nervous and worn out with having to drag around to parties and be nice to all your friends, and look as if I'm a happy woman, when all you do, whenever we're alone, is storm and scowl at me, the way you're doing now!"

"Stella, I want to know who started this story."

"Oh, for heaven's sake!" she cried angrily. "Do you think I'm going to sit up all night and talk about your old Mrs. Gliesinger? If you've got to go on ranting about her, go outdoors and rant about her to yourself; you can't rant about her any longer to me, because I'm going to try and get a little sleep." And with that, her other preparations being now completed, she pulled down the bed, shook out the pillows, and promptly placed herself under the covers. "Good-night!" she said conclusively.

William had begun to pace the floor. "I intend to find out what's going on," he insisted doggedly.

"I've always felt sorry for anybody that had stories going around about their domestic life; it always seemed to me to kind of disgrace 'em, and I never dreamed such a thing could happen to me. I'm going to find out what started——"

She interrupted him sharply. "How long do you propose to keep that light shining straight in my eyes?"

"Stella, I propose to find out how this story got started."

With her eyes tightly closed, Stella began to hum loudly the air of "Auld Lang Syne"; and, when he repeated, with increasing sternness, that he was determined to discover the origin of the misinformation that had stimulated Mrs. Gliesinger to offer him advice, his recumbent wife made her humming more coherent; she began to sing the words of the song.

This overcame William; she was too much for him, and he sat down upon the foot of the bed, taking his baffled head in his hands. "You talk about dragging around to parties and trying to look happy. I guess I've had to be doing my share of that! How do you think I felt to-night when Mrs. Gliesinger let it out to me what must be going all around the N.K.U.? Once a story like that gets started there's no telling what twists they won't put on it or where it'll end. Lord knows when it'll reach the Big Boss, himself! Pretty nearly everything does get to him, in one shape or another, before it stops. For all I know, it may have got to him already, and I certainly don't feel like going up there to-morrow night. It makes me feel just sick, as if I couldn't face anybody for fear of what they're thinking about me."

Stella had continued to sing "Auld Lang Syne"; but a part of what he was saying caught her attention sharply. She opened her eyes. "Going up where to-morrow night?"

"To the Big Boss's to dinner."

"Who is?"

"We are."

"What?" she almost shouted, and abruptly sat up straight in bed. "What are you talking about?"

"We've got to go," William said dismally. "I didn't feel much like it when he asked me, and I certainly feel a whole lot less like it, now. He said he wanted us to come up to his house for Sunday evening dinner, because he thought on account of our new relation it'd be pleasant to establish a little more personal intimacy between us. That was the way he——"

"When did he ask you?"

"This morning."

"He told you this morning!" Stella cried angrily. "Why didn't you tell me before? Why didn't you telephone me instantly?"

"What? I didn't think of it. But anyhow, Stella, you've got me so that I hardly dare to say anything to you about anything. We'd been almost not speaking at all, and, when you're hardly speaking to a person, it's not very liable to occur to you to be calling him up on the telephone."

"I think that's the flimsiest excuse I ever heard any man mean enough to make in my life!" She was furious. "You've known it all day and you wait until after midnight to tell me, and to-morrow's Sunday! And then you come ranting around to me, wondering how the story's got around that you're jealous. If you haven't given the trickiest, most treacherous exhibition of it——"

"Of what?" William asked aghast. "Of jealousy? In the name of heaven, what am I jealous of?"

"Of your wife's success!" she shouted, fairly in his face. "You didn't tell me until now because you want to make me look cheap, and in your mean little heart, Bill Greeley, you know it!"

"I want to make you look cheap?"

"Yes, you do! If you'd called me up even this morning I could have got Aurelia and hurried down town and found something that would have been at least half decent to wear!" She jumped out of bed, ran to the closet where she kept her clothes and began to rummage through her dresses, continuing meanwhile to upbraid him fiercely. "It never occurred to you to call me up; no, I guess it didn't! You wanted me to go up there to meet the best dressed people in this town and have them all thinking that I look like Bennettsville, didn't you? Well, I guess you've got your way; that's what I'll look like! I haven't got a single evening dress fit to wear to anything better than sloppy, third-class parties like the one your friends gave us to-night."

"You haven't? Why, what's the matter with that blue one you wore at my inauguration banquet?"

"*Your* inauguration banquet! Oh, my!" She hooted at him. "Talk some more about that; I like to hear you!"

"Well, what's the matter with that dress?"

"I wore it!" she shouted. "I wore it at the *banquet!* I'd rather go to that dinner to-morrow night in a wrapper, and I expect that'd prob'ly suit you perfectly. You've done your best to get me up there looking like a scarecrow, and I don't want to hear any more from you. Get off the bed." She began to bring dresses from the closet and to dispose them upon the bed for inspection. "Get off that bed and go sit somewheres else. Not on the *sofa!*" She cried at him shrilly, as he moved in that direction. "And not at my dressing table, either. Good heavens! When you've done a thing like this to me can't you even keep out of my way?"

It was William who finally, with the tables reversed, begged for the chance to slumber that night. Stella, accompanying her researches with reiterated murmurs of reproach and allowing him small opportunities for either plaintive explanation or dismal repartee, busily continued to flurry among all the items of her wardrobe, until at last he drowsed in a stiff chair with his head against the wall. Not until after three o'clock did she let him get to bed; and, when he woke in the morning she was already up and had gone to Aurelia with her problem.

XI

THE question of selection from their joint wardrobes occupied the two ladies most of the day; William was turned out of his apartment; and all afternoon he and Mr. Hedge drove apathetically through the city's parks and about the suburbs, while their wives, at home, remained in diligent conference. Aurelia and Stella scissored and sewed, mumbled to each other feverishly with pins in their mouths, and, in their tensest moments, examined the result of their work as Stella anxiously posed before the mirror, trying on one transformed vesture after another. It was not until after sunset that the decision was made in favor of an afternoon dress of Stella's from which the sleeves, the shoulders, a generous section of material in front between the shoulders and, at the back, a triangular piece extending down to the waist, had been removed. This lively garment of figured pale green silk came just to Stella's knees, and Aurelia devised for it a vivid ornamentation. She had a rhinestone girdle, which she cheerfully dismembered and used to make an edging at the neck and down the back and two little glittering straps over the shoulders. Stella owned a sunburst of false diamonds, and with this they caught the dress up a little at her hip. They chose silver-colored stockings and the silvered shoes with rhinestone buckles that Stella had worn at the banquet—she might risk this much repetition without fear of detection, they felt.

Finally then, Stella stood silently before the mirror with this extemporized costume completed upon her; but Aurelia went into raptures. "You're it! Stella, you're absolutely it! You can walk into that house absolutely self-confident because he's going to fall flat at your feet the minute he sees you!" She laughed joyously. "Don't you have one second's worry or fear; you're the whole N.K.U. works to-night! You'll see! It's going to be a bigger night for you than even the banquet was; you're going to just walk right over everything!"

Stella, fascinated, had not taken her eyes from the mirror during the last half hour. "What about just a touch more color?"

"For your face? Just a shade more; but not on your lips. Your lips are exactly right." Aurelia applied the rouge herself. "There, and don't you touch it again."

"No," Stella said in a hushed voice. "It certainly does look right."

"Right? I'll tell the world! You know, yourself, you never saw such a picture as you make right now in all your life!"

"I guess I never did," Stella said almost in a whisper, and her entranced eyes grew dreamy. "I guess I have to admit it, Aurelia; I guess, after all, it even beats the cornflower chiffon. I thought I'd wear my crystal earrings, but I don't believe I need one more touch."

"Yes, you do but not any earrings. I've just had one last big idea. When those two men come back again I guess we'll have to let 'em in, because Bill made such a fuss about getting a chance to do his own dressing the last time he came hammering on the door that we can't keep him out much longer. Well, we'll let him get started—he can take his clothes in the bathroom, and Henry can run an errand for us. The Boulevard Flower Shop is open on Sunday, and we'll send Henry to get a bunch of orchids for you as exactly like the one Mr. Cooper sent you for the banquet as they can make up into a corsage. That ought to let him know you aren't so hard-hearted that you haven't been doing a little thinking about him, Stell'!"

"Who?" Stella asked. "Henry?" And, upon this sally, the two joined in a short burst of laughter; they calmed themselves quickly. "I never felt so excited in all my life!" Stella said.

"Who wouldn't be? Think what's happening!"

"Aurelia, after I get there, what do you think I better talk about?"

"I guess you won't have any trouble about that," Aurelia returned archly. "You'll be sitting next to him, of course, so just go on with what you were talking about with him at the banquet."

"Yes, but that's the trouble. You see, we didn't talk much about any one special thing that night. He paid me all those compliments I told you about; but the whole world was staring at us, and the Mayor kept breaking in and talking to him and——"

"I guess he said enough!"

"Yes, but I do wonder how I'd better begin to-night, after we get at the table. For instance——"

"For instance," Aurelia interrupted, with burlesque gravity, "you might ask him how much of an invalid the flu has made Mrs. Cooper, and whether she really is going to get well or not."

"Oh, you wouldn't——"

"No, I certainly wouldn't," Aurelia returned, greatly amused. Then she became more serious. "If I were in your place, I wouldn't bother much talking about the weather just to get going; I'd start right in. Just about the first thing I'd say, I'd say it was just perfectly wonderful how he didn't have any gray in his hair. I'd say that of course I didn't mean on account of his age; but, with all his cares and worries over being the president of such an enormous business, anybody would have expected that he'd be kind of more worn-out looking, so to speak. Then I'd just sort of laugh, as if I didn't mean it *too* much in earnest and was only half-joking, as it were, and put in something a little more serious about how I always did like distinguished looking men."

Stella was impressed. "That's just about what I thought I would do. I think that's just about the way I'll start things off, Aurelia. I'm all right, once I get going; I know that."

"Oh, you're certain to get going; and when you get going really good, Stella, you're absolutely great. When you get that way there isn't anything on earth you can't get away with; and, for heaven's sake, don't forget about the raise for Henry! The sooner we put that over, the better."

"You needn't be afraid about that," Stella said lightly. "It's almost the first thing I intend to put over to-night. I'm going to have you in a house just as near ours as we can get it. Do you think I ought to hint anything definite about what salary'll be needed for——"

"No," Aurelia returned thoughtfully, "not exactly in so many words. Just something about how he might feel about doing the right thing in kind of a big way, and how terribly it would please you to see your friends fixed up near you and everything. Just feel it out a little as you go along, and then shoot for it, you know, Stella."

"Oh, I'll shoot for it!" Stella, looking at the mirror, laughed exultantly and missed nothing of the lovely imaged laughter she saw there. "And I'll bring it down, too!" she cried, not to Aurelia but to the reproduced beauty before her.

Time was, and not long ago at that, when Aurelia knew spiteful moments for the joy Stella had of her mirror; but now the little confidante had no jealousy left within her; she was vehement in purest admiration. "You just make me gasp, Stella Greeley!" she burst forth. "You ought to've been born a queen! You are one; yes you are, and you're going to be queen of the N.K.U.! That's certain! There isn't anything on earth you can't do."

They believed it; Stella's radiance enveloped them both and they seemed to share it;—intoxicated, they saw in it the bright necromancy that was to bring them each her heart's desire, and it was opon this mood of exaltation that the hammering of William's knuckles upon the door, and his insistent demand for entrance, came as a warning that the great hour was near at hand. They let him come in and turned him into the bathroom with his arms full of clothes while Aurelia spoke hurriedly with her husband who had lingered in the corridor, and bade him make haste to be gone for the orchids; but he hesitated.

"I was just thinking," he said slowly, "there was something I wanted to tell you, Aurelia. At any rate, I was going to tell Bill about it this afternoon, but then I thought I'd wait till we got home where all four of us could sort of sit down and talk it over, you and Stella and Bill and I. I thought it'd be a good time to do it now, so if Stella's got her clothes on I'll just come in and——"

"Come in? What for?"

"Why, to talk this thing over that I was going to tell you and Stella and Bill about. If we could all four just sit down——"

"My heavens!" Aurelia uttered a cry of impatience and pushed him toward the door of the elevator shaft. "Go on. You've got just about twenty-five minutes to get back here from The Boulevard Flower Shop with those orchids for Stella. Go on."

"But——"

"Go on! I never knew such a man!"

"All right," he said wanly, "I guess I might as well." And, as he departed down the corridor, Aurelia ran back to the brilliant figure still standing entranced before the mirror.

"Stella, did you ever in your life! You heard what the poor old bonehead said, didn't you? Wanting to come in here now and 'sit down and talk things over'! Isn't that like a man?"

"And isn't that?" Stella cried merrily, with a gesture of her golden head toward the bathroom door which imperfectly muffled explosive words; William had evidently lost something beneath the bathtub.

The two young wives made the room ring with their happy and excited laughter; and Aurelia began to circle in a merry little dance about her friend. "Bow to the Queen!" she sang. "Kiss the King's hand and bow to the Queen! Bow to the fairest you've ever seen! Bow to the Queen! Bow to the Queen!"

XII

THE gray stone terrace, where the Greeleys stood in the dark twilight waiting for admission outside of a deeply vestibuled oaken door, had an air dimly majestic that was a little daunting to William, but not in the least so to Stella. Aforetime, she had often driven by here and looked in almost tremulously at the long and massive house set far back, among shrubberies and high trees, at the end of a green lawn so broad, so costly, so groomed that even to imagine herself crossing it, or guiding her rattling little car up the driveway that bordered it, made her gasp. That time seemed now to her a long, long while ago. Fresh from her mirror and Aurelia, she was full-panoplied in a dauntless self-confidence that laughed pityingly at all such former absurd timidities; she could almost feel herself glittering under her wrap; the dusk seemed warm with gold that shone through the wisp of chiffon she had wound about her head, and, proudly and consciously wearing this glitter and this gold, she found within herself a new and triumphant personality equal to anything and not afraid of lawns or terraces—less still of such pompous and showy ladies as might be revealed by the opening of the oaken door. Only one thing annoyed her.

"You had plenty of time, yesterday, to have done the right thing," she said to William. "You could just as well have looked up to the minute as not, even if you had to buy a full evening dress suit ready-made. You saw Mr. Cooper at the banquet with a tail coat, pearl studs, white vest, white necktie, and everything."

"He was the only one," William protested nervously.

"He won't be the only one here. You'll be the only one—the only one in a tuck!"

"I can't help it now," he said desperately. "Oh, golly! I wish these next three hours were over and we were——"

"Be quiet!" she whispered imperiously.

She had expected the door to be opened by a liveried figure defined in her mind as an "English butler"; instead, the office was performed by a colored man of affable appearance.

"Uh— Howdy-do! Is Mr. Cooper at home this

evening?" William inquired, and coughed. "Anyhow, he invited us to——" But Stella swept by him and into the broad hall. "Mr. and Mrs. William Greeley," she announced haughtily.

"Yes, sir." The colored man smiled hospitably. "He home. Come right in, sir; come right in." William obeyed, and, entering, found Stella already delivering her wrap and chiffon scarf to a negro maid. "Thank you," he said to the man, as the latter took his overcoat and soft hat. "Much obliged! Much obliged!"

Stella, who said nothing to the maid, sent him a quick, scornful glance over her shoulder; then the two followed the colored man to a wide, open doorway and passed through it into a large, shadowy room, where, in the illumination of a couple of shaded table lamps and a fire crackling under a carved stone mantel, seven or eight people were talking quietly. In this soft and mellow light and against the altering brown shadows, the marble and rose and green and gold of Stella, gleaming brilliants, were startling; her instant feeling was that of an overwhelming superiority to the other women present. Her first impression of them was not of their faces but of their clothes—silks and silk crêpes of dark blue, brown, gray and black with a little embroidery and dull colored decoration; and all of them with sleeves. Before she had time to take detailed or individual note of these obscurely revealed ladies she sweepingly classified them in a group, and, with exultation and yet with disappointment, too, set them down as unimportant and rather dowdy.

Cooper came forward cordially, and the nervous William perceived that his own short coat and black tie were reassuringly of the mode adopted by his host and the other gentlemen present. "I'm delighted to see you, Mr. Greeley. Mrs. Greeley, this is very good of you. I want you to meet Mrs. Cooper."

Mrs. Cooper had followed him. She was thin and straight, tall and of a reticent yet not ungracious presence; her hair, not short, showed faintly gray; her gray eyes were observant and withholding, and upon her fine lips there was, as if habitually, a thin, somewhat preoccupied smile. "How d'you do, Mrs. Greeley," she said in a voice surprising for its vibrant contralto richness, and she turned to William. "Mr. Greeley, I think it's high time I should have the pleasure of meeting you—my husband's told me so much about you. I can't tell you what a pleasure it is to have you here."

But Cooper was already setting the party in motion; Henry Hedge had been slow with the orchids, and the Greeleys were late. Panelled doors were thrown open upon a brightly lighted dining room, and there, at the round table where old silver gleamed upon a cloth of lace, Stella found that her seat was, as she and Aurelia had confidently expected, next to her host's; but it was upon his left. There, too, glancing across the table, she was startled to find herself looking straight into the dark, intelligent eyes of Miss Crystal Nelson. No personal intelligence of Stella, however, shone at just this moment in the glance of that capable young woman;—Miss Nelson appeared to be unaware of the ocular contact and her gaze to be merely in passage and on its way to rest upon Mrs. Cooper. Evidently, a discussion between these two ladies had been interrupted by the arrival of the Greeleys and the migration of the party to the table; for Miss Nelson said, with some crispness:

"Don't rest upon the complacent assurance that you convince me. The *scherzo* was by far the worst executed thing on their whole program."

Mrs. Cooper shook her head. "Ansonini didn't think so, and, as he composed it himself——"

Miss Nelson took the words from her mouth. "As he composed it himself he was the last person to be able to judge. A composer, conducting, can always hear his meanings into the sounds he evokes from his musicians; and that's dangerous. It's the weakness of a conducting composer as volatile as Ansonini to believe that he has made his meanings come out of the music simply because he's been able to hear them into it, himself."

"Are you laying down a law?" Mrs. Cooper inquired spiritedly. "Composers should never conduct?"

"That isn't implied in what I said," Miss Nelson returned. "Mr. Leahart, you'll have to continue to act as referee. Is it fair for her to assume there was any such implication?"

Her appeal was to the person at Stella's left, a dry, sallow, wisp-bearded man with a head like Don Quixote's. "No," he said seriously. "Laura has no right to hear any such meaning into your own conducting of this argument, Crystal; and you're entirely correct. But I'm not going to act as your referee any longer; I can find something much pleasanter to do in talking to Mrs. Greeley." He turned to Stella. "Mrs. Greeley, they haven't been kind enough to make me known to you, but my name is Leahart; that's my wife upon Mr. Cooper's right. Mrs. Cooper and Miss Nelson have been boring me very much with their old Ansonini and a 'modernist' concert Mrs. Cooper had here this afternoon. I detest the whole school; and I have only one word for the movement, whether it be in literature, music, painting or sculpture, and my word is 'Blah'! What is your feeling? Could you say the word with me?"

Stella bent upon him a gaze of profound inquiry. "Say 'Blah'?"

But Cooper prevented Mr. Leahart from replying. "You know perfectly well, Leahart, that Mrs. Cooper doesn't allow conversations *a duo* at our Sunday evening table. Besides, Mrs. Greeley, he'll smother you with Bach and he won't stop to find out first whether you're a Bach worshipper as he is or not; he won't even care whether you have any interest in music at all or not. They're a terrible couple, these Leaharts." He addressed the table at large. "It seems to me a dreadful thing that a Brahms enthusiast like Mrs. Leahart should have for a husband a Bach maniac. Bach maniacs make themselves priests of a religion. For them, if you wander from Bach, it is all '*à bas*' and '*conspuez*.' Brahms enthusiasts are not quite so mad; their Brahmsitic wildness knows temperate moments when it is able to admit that there have been other composers, and even that there may be such a thing as a composer who is not a dead man." Here he turned again, for the moment to Stella, explaining, "My wife, Miss Nelson and I are of the catholic party; we believe in great dead men and are gratefully aware that the music of the Seventeenth Century did not consist entirely of Louis the Thirteenth's gavotte, nor that of the Eighteenth Century of the jackdawings of Rouget de Lisle; but for us enthusiasm really begins with Debussy."

"Enthusiasm!" Leahart exclaimed, and he emitted a derisive cackle. "There are two people present who spent forty-eight hours on sleeping cars going to and coming from the audition of a new symphony; they argued every minute of the way; one of them caught a cold that laid her by the heels for a fortnight; and the symphony was one that could have been furnished them here at home at any time by the slight exertion of driving to a boiler factory. You call me a maniac, and yet these two persons would do the same thing again for the same purpose and with the same result. I ask you!"

Mrs. Cooper nodded emphatically. "Certainly, we would! Arguing with Crystal for two solid days is worth a cold anytime, not to speak of the symphony, which was magnificent. Ask my husband. He'd heard it and would have gone with us to hear it again if business hadn't kept him at home. We'd all three go again, and probably shall the next time it's given. We argue, yes; it's a great pleasure, for basically we are in unison."

"Yes," Cooper agreed. "We are like George Raymond here; he is horribly bored by everything musical; his ears are large, but atrophied because he has never had any use for them; he cares for nothing except what comes through the eye. Our likeness to him is this: that he admits Velasquez and Goya and el Greco but gets really excited only about Matisse."

Mr. George Raymond, a young man of ruddy and amiable countenance offered quick protest. "No, no! If I didn't do more than 'admit' Velasquez I'd think you might well enough say I had atrophied eyes, as well as atrophied ears. I don't merely 'admit' him; I proclaim him, and proclaim him the greatest; but I'm able to see something in Matisse, too."

At this, the dry and thin Leahart suffered himself to utter one short and sharp yelp of laughter. "Good

heavens! Matisse! Picasso! Gaugin! Oh, dearie me!"
He turned for sympathy to the glittering figure beside him. "Mrs. Greeley, do we have to stand this?"

For reply, Stella smiled, trying to impart to her
expression an air of knowing archness, and this
seemed to suffice Mr. Leahart.

"If it weren't for Mrs. Leahart and me," he said,
"you might be led to suppose you'd stumbled upon a
circle of 'modernist' lunatics. Don't be deceived,
Mrs. Greeley; they delude themselves, and they do
not like what they praise. Cooper, for instance. He
thinks he likes 'modernism' in art, but you'll observe
he has none of it on his walls. However, he's more
inconsistent than that: he has two personalities.
Here, in this semi-domestic circle of his, he spends a
great deal of time 'talking art,' as you've heard; he's
'precious,' highfalutin, a descendant of Petronius
apparently, or perhaps only an aesthetic suburban
squire."

But Cooper, laughing cheerfully, objected. "What
is this? Steele in the *Spectator* building up a 'charac-
ter' to be guessed at?"

"If you like," Leahart responded calmly. "He's a
curious fellow, this Cooper—or rather I should say
these Coopers, for there are two of him; I've seen the

other one upon a few occasions when he has lured me to view him in operation upon the scene of his odious commercial exploits. Those terrible tracts covered with glass and concrete and known to their own thousands of unfortunates as the 'N.K.U.' He even got me to sit on the platform with him there once and hear him introduce a lecturer he had imported to edify his suffering employees. There was a Cooper totally a stranger to me, an unfamiliar, speaking an unfamiliar tongue; incarnately a Rotarian. I suppose he spoke to those people in the lingo they understand; and perhaps he feels it necessary to be, among them, the kind of potentate they comprehend; but on the other hand the N.K.U. Cooper may be the real one and this champion of *art nouveau*, the counterfeit. I'll appeal to Mr. Greeley for light on the problem. Mr. Greeley, you're one of those very unfortunates I've just mentioned; you're naturally familiar with the N.K.U. Cooper and you now behold him in his domestic, aesthetic aspect, a wholly different creature. Which, in your judgment, is the veritable?"

William, who had grown red instantly upon being addressed, became redder as the smiling attention of the table centered upon him. He coughed, produced from an inner pocket a neatly folded handkerchief, shook it out, wiped his forehead, coughed again; then said with some huskiness, "Well, if I get you—I mean if you mean Mr. Cooper's the whole works at the N.K.U., why, he certainly is, and a man who's the whole works on that job would be pretty likely to be the whole works at anything else he tackled like—like talking art as you were saying, for instance, Mr. Leahart." William seemed to gain a little confidence as he went on. "Everybody in the N.K.U. knows Mr. Cooper is a man that puts himself into anything he does; if you listen to him talking about machinery you think he's an engineer; but then again when he's talking distribution you think he must be a salesman. That's one way to tell a big man from an average man; if you got Mr. Cooper to talking medicine, for instance, a stranger would probably take him for a doctor."

This speech met with a success amazing to both the speaker and his wife. There was a murmur of applausive laughter and Leahart clapped his thin yellow hands together.

"Bravo!" he said. "You live up to your reputation, Mr. Greeley. Just before your arrival here, Miss Nelson and Mr. Cooper were telling us that in addition to having precisely the executive genius they found wanting in your predecessors in office you had recently shown a capacity for analysis such as you've just proved you indeed possess. They were telling us of your adroit oratory upon the occasion of some species of commercial feast or banquet when you——"

William was unable not to interrupt. "Oh, murder!" he exclaimed, and looked pathetically at his host. "I don't suppose I'll ever be able to live it down."

"I hope not," Cooper returned genially. "Leahart's in earnest, Greeley. What we were talking about was your instinctively and in all sincerity finding exactly what was the most adroit thing for you to say under the circumstances. Your speech placated all those officials of longer service who naturally had some jealousy of you for being passed over their heads, and helped to prove the native capacity I'd marked in you for handling men." He turned to Leahart. "I'm glad Greeley's explanation of me satisfies you and I'm prepared to admit that just as you are incarnately a Bach maniac so am I what I've often been called, an N.K.U. fanatic—that is when I'm on N.K.U. ground."

Leahart laughed. "And that's wherever you tread!

Mr. Greeley is right: if you were talking medicine, a stranger might think you a doctor; but if he listened closely he'd find you were prescribing concoctions brewed in N.K.U. utensils, and the real reason you enthuse over 'modernist' music, like that horrible new Soviet symphony, is that it might just as well be made by your own sledge hammers and aluminum boilers and dynamos and steam whistles as by violins, 'cellos, brasses, drums and cymbals. After all, you see—" he turned quizzically to Stella—"for all your husband's applauded powers of analysis he's mistaken; that's because of his loyalty to his chief, of course, a virtue that one perceives he carries to the most fantastic extremes. Can you bear it, Mrs. Greeley? Do you permit so much diversion of worship to a deity I'm positive he did not mention when he took his marital vows? I was unable to persuade you to say 'Blah' to modernism with me, but here is a subject that must elicit from you some expression of natural indignation; I am sure that you will speak."

Stella stared in utter blankness at this terrible old man whom she already began to hate; she had been afraid that he would turn to her again with another of his inexplicable questions. She had only the vaguest and most clouded perception of his meaning now—

but it was clear that he, and the rest of the little company as well, expected a reply from her, and, as a defense against what seemed to her an unfamiliar form of hostile raillery, she fell back upon the kind of light mockery of which Aurelia had prophesied such great things in case Stella should "get going" at this vital little dinner party.

"Isn't he the high-brow cut-up, though?" she said to Cooper loudly but in the manner of one intimate joker to another. "I'll tell the world!" And, as was her habit when she spoke humorously, she followed up her jocosity with a peal of corroborative laughter.

For a moment the hearty sound of her own voice in laughter reassured her, and she seemed to have passed a crisis successfully; but she had the misfortune to laugh alone. Therefore, she continued her hilarity as if in the hope of inspiring others to join her; then she stopped abruptly. Cooper, whose coat sleeve she had ventured to touch in a gesture customary with her when she emphasized a joke, was looking at her strangely, and slowly his face reddened though he made some indulgent sounds as of a courtesy laughter. But a hush had come upon the table; gravity prevailed in all expressions there; tension was felt, and then the crackling voice of Leahart relieved it.

"So little success," he said, "have ever I had with the fair! Mrs. Greeley is right, and my wife bestowed her hand upon me only to win an argument in which I held the affirmative that she wouldn't." Upon this, someone laughed nervously and then, as it seemed, most of the small party began to talk at once, and rapidly.

XIII

STELLA, however, was not one of the talkers; when the vocal tokens of her merriment had ceased she still contrived to retain upon her face the contours of laughter, and thus strove to appear unconscious that her reprisal upon the incomprehensible Leahart had not proved a great comedy success. Gradually, this expression of hilarity relapsed into what she intended for a smile of reminiscent amusement; but the smile was a little like the jauntily flown flag of an ammunitionless citadel under fire and unable to reply. She wished to join in the conversation now suddenly become lively; she tried to think of witticisms to be flung right and left among these people who apparently had no sense of humor and misunderstood her effort to "get going." But the needed witticisms remained elusive and she could only sit silent, suffering more and more with the knowledge that her fixed smile was becoming glassier and glassier.

At the outset of this dinner party she had perceived that the evening was not going to be what she and Aurelia had so confidently and thrillingly expected; the word *scherzo* sprang from a vocabulary appalling to her, and this word upon the lips of Miss Crystal Nelson, just after the company had sat down, was almost as startling to her as the very presence of Miss Nelson, herself, familiarly and intimately in this house. Other words not less discomfiting than *scherzo* had followed—phrases and concatenations of sound meaningless to her, and outrageous names seeming to belong to remote foreign celebrities of whom she had never heard anything and never wished to hear anything. Now the talk seemed to whirl and eddy more confusingly than ever about her self-conscious head as with admirable spirit she sought to maintain her smile and wear the air of a superior person bored by all this prattle, yet polite about it. She fell back upon every reassurance she could get hold of; far beyond any possible comparison, she was the best looking woman present, and, what was almost equally important, she felt, she was also incomparably the best dressed—indeed the only one with a perfect pretension to smartness. Let these others go on with their high-brow palaverings, she thought: what need a woman who was actually a

Beauty care? Nevertheless, she did care; she hated
the high-brow talk—it was all pose and show-off and
bunk anyhow—but, as it went on, she began to feel
not only excluded but overwhelmed by it.

Indomitably, she sat facing it with her frozen smile,
and, at intervals, found some relief in bending a little
over her plate, seeming to engage herself with food
that was tasteless to her, while within her a proud
heart held steadfast her resolution to be scornful.
Then suddenly she was visited by a terrible doubt.
Her dreadful and loquacious neighbor, the detested
Leahart, had been making what appeared to be something in the nature of an address, and, so far as Stella's comprehension was concerned, he might as well
have been speaking in a foreign tongue, when, for a
moment or two, he became all too easily intelligible.

"Such a passage in a work of the highest literary
pretension," he said, "is as shocking as Chopin's
pretty sentimentality in the midst of his *Marche
Funèbre*. It is like a ballet girl at a prayer meeting of
mountaineers; it is a false note, like a pretty woman
overdressed at a quiet party. It is like a rococo
frame upon a Fra Angelico; it is like——"

But Stella heard him no further. He was entirely
innocent; he had not thought of her; far less had he

any wish to avenge himself upon her for her too sprightly sally; nevertheless, the words "like a pretty woman overdressed at a quiet party" rang spitefully in her ears. Unreasonably (and disastrously for her already perturbed self-esteem) she thought he had intended a wicked, sideling jibe. "Overdressed!" Was that what these high-brow snobs were daring to think of her? She lifted her head haughtily and sent a challenging glance about the table; but everyone was listening eagerly to Leahart who continued to be voluble; even William seemed to be interested in his crazy talk and to have some comprehension of it. No one was paying the slightest attention to her; and, for all she apparently counted with these people, she might as well have been sitting at home, still unknown to them, in her kitchenette apartment at the Warwicke Armes. "Overdressed!" The sting of the intolerable word went deeper and deeper. Why did these people so suavely exclude her? If only the women were treating her as an outsider she could have understood it as their offensive defense against a competitor of superior charm; but the men left her as completely outside the circle as did the women, and it was a man who had so slyly insulted her. "Overdressed!" Could it possibly be true?

When that fear came upon her she began to be stricken. She saw that at least from the point of view of "these people" it was true, and she was over-dressed; she and Aurelia had made a terrible mistake. And with this, the smile she had worn so long became not merely glassy but piteously vacant; it was now not the jaunty flag of a still defiant fortalice but the white emblem of defeat fluttering over a pillaged city. Dazed, Stella began to have a dim perception that the "high-brow" talk of "these people" was their habitual means of expression, and that although so far as she was concerned it was a foreign language, yet it was the only one they spoke. Even if they had wished to include her they had no more power to do so than she had to speak to them in their own tongue; through the diabolic Leahart, they had made at-tempts at communication, but her replies, "say Blah?" and "Isn't he the high-brow cut-up?" had proved to them that their experiment was a failure. Moreover, there was painful significance in the fact that it was not Cooper who had made the experiment.

She had only half comprehended Leahart's whimsi-cal characterization of his friend, yet she was now acquiring an uncomfortably clear realization of the two aspects of Cooper, and she perceived that at his

own table and among his own familiars he wore his
true and natural manner. With this, there vanished
the last shred of feeble pretense to herself that on
account of the presence of Mrs. Cooper he had not
deemed it wise to continue the attitude of gallantry
that had marked him at the banquet. Then had that
attitude of gallantry, itself, been only a part of his
N.K.U. aspect, assumed as a good paternal policy?
"Soft-soaping!" she thought bitterly, thus describing
to herself the display of a newly promoted factory
manager's wife for N.K.U. emulation. Had the "Big
Boss" indeed thought of her all along merely in that
capacity—the wife of his deserving factotum? Since
she came into his house to-night he had not asked her
a question or addressed to her a remark that gave her
a chance to reply: evidently, he had expected nothing
from her, and had already thought of her what
"these people" thought of her now, that she was an
outsider! Then why had he invited her?

Her beautiful, long brown eyelashes shadowed
Stella's eyes as she bent her head above her plate,
then lifted, and she sent round the table a slow and
sullen glance that came to rest upon the face of her
husband. William was not having a bad time at all;
he had just replied to a question of Mrs. Cooper's,

and evidently with some credit, for everyone except his wife was laughing amiably. He could communicate with "these people," it seemed, and they with him. Was he the reason his wife had been asked to sit in exile at this feast?

Stella felt that she hated him; she hated only one person more, but this greater hatred was not because of any wifely jealousy, for she had no need to feel that sort of jealousy now, and she knew it. The most talkative person at the table, even surpassing Leahart, had become Miss Crystal Nelson; and it was for her easy and comfortable manner in this overpowering house, for the applause she met, and for her assured place among "these people" that Stella hated her. Crystal talked on gayly; she was merry, and it was apparent that the others even thought her sparkling, for sometimes Mrs. Cooper clapped her hands, while Leahart and Cooper cried "Bravo!"

Stella drove her knife into a slice of partridge as if she stabbed it; she felt that she must die of chagrin unless she shouted, "Oh, shut up! You're nothing but my husband's old maid secretary! So shut up!"

XIV

FOR coffee the gentlemen remained at the table, smoking, while the ladies withdrew to a room of palatial spaciousness with walls painted a faded apple-green and an elaborately colored, panelled ceiling upheld by tall pilasters of dull gold. The faintly gleaming parquetry floor had no rugs and at one end of the room were two magnificent pianos of the type recognizable to Stella as "concert grand"; but the lustrous darkness of these two great, cold shapes was warmed by a glowing presence near them. An old Venetian cabinet, lofty and capacious, showed forth in a faded gorgeousness that once had been too gay in red and green and blue and gold; but now was happily mellowed by a couple of centuries; and it was to this receptacle that Mrs. Cooper led Mrs. Leahart and Mrs. Raymond, the wife of the ruddy young man who liked Matisse.

"I'll show you two those missals my husband spoke of having collected," the hostess said, "and those old loose sheets of Gregorian Chants. Crystal knows them by heart and she and I have tried to play them over together any number of times. Besides, she must be about ready to stretch herself out on two chairs, I should think, after the dissertation she gave us upon the relation of folk songs to jazz. Help me, will you?" As she spoke, she began to take from the cabinet heavy old volumes bound in brown, and ponderous portfolios stuffed with yellowed sheets of music; the two ladies assisted her to spread these out upon a table, and then, seating themselves beside it, began to examine the music and to chatter busily among themselves, a group sufficiently detached.

Stella, at the other end of the room, thought that she had been purposely left to herself, and for a moment this seemed the last straw; then she perceived that she had not been left to herself but in the care of Miss Crystal Nelson.

"Let's sit down where we can't even hear them," Crystal said affably, and, alluding to a chair that she pushed toward the stiff and staring guest, she continued, "There, that was made in the reign of a dainty, old French king, and it looks charmingly appropriate to you." She moved another chair close to it and set a slim table between them. "We can put our coffee on that, when it comes, and be quite comfortable. Shan't we sit down?" Then, as she set the example suggested and Stella followed it, she laughed. "Laura Cooper, over there, is perfectly happy showing those women thousands of little black squares made by a lot of old monks as notes for the musical scale. I'm glad this room's sixty feet long, aren't you? I do think we've had about enough music for one evening, and I'd rather talk N.K.U. for a change, wouldn't you, Mrs. Greeley?"

"Not necessarily," Stella returned. "I guess I don't have to talk about the N.K.U., Miss Nelson. There *are* a few other subjects I'm familiar with, I believe."

Her tone was not encouraging; but Crystal Nelson showed no sign of being repelled by it. "Laura's a dear, of course," she said. "And so is he, too, for that matter. Such warm-hearted, kindly, real people! They're tremendously interested in your husband, Mrs. Greeley, and so is everybody else in the N.K.U., naturally. We all feel proud of him that he's made such a splendid start in his new position; but then, of course, we all knew that he was just the man for it, Mr. Cooper particularly, because he's been watching Mr. Greeley for a long time, always with increasing faith in him. You must be immensely proud of him, Mrs. Greeley."

This assumption was too much for Stella; she was unable to fall in with it. "Me! Proud of him?" she said coldly. "Oh, I don't know."

"But of course you are," the smiling Crystal assured her warmly. "You're just putting on airs with me about it, Mrs. Greeley."

"What!"

"Of course you're proud of him," Crystal insisted, and she laughed placatively. "Here's your coffee." And then, when the two small cups had been placed upon the table, and the colored man who brought them had withdrawn, she laughed again. "Mr. Greeley's so good, so simple and true, and yet so tremendously intelligent and energetic in his work that I know in your heart you feel——"

But Stella was unable to contain herself any longer. "You don't! You don't know anything about what I feel in my heart. I wouldn't be very likely to show anything I felt in a place like this, and before the kind of people Mr. Cooper's got here to-night, would I?" And she turned toward Crystal a hot face; angry tears stood in her eyes. "Would anybody show what was in their heart before such a lot of high-brow, frozen-face——"

"Mrs. Greeley!" Crystal leaned forward, protest-

ing in a gentle voice. "It's too bad; but I was afraid
you felt a little like that. You mustn't——"

"Why mustn't I? What have you got to do with
it?"

"You poor thing," Crystal said, and her tone was
so patently one of genuine and friendly compassion
that Stella listened. "You mustn't think it of us, Mrs.
Greeley. I've just told you that Mr. and Mrs.
Cooper are the kindest-hearted people in the world.
They're immensely happy and congenial in their life
together, as anyone who comes into the house can
see immediately; but they spare a great deal of time
from their own happiness and put themselves to no
end of trouble to do kind things for other people.
They'd both be terribly distressed to think you'd
been having a wretched evening, and I'm sure you
won't let them see it."

"It's nobody's business what kind of an evening I'm
having," Stella said in a fierce, low voice. "It certainly isn't yours." Then suddenly, and to her own
horror, she sniffled, with trembling fingers she began
to fumble at her dress.

Seeing her need, Crystal slipped a handkerchief into
her hand. "Turn away just a little," she whispered.
"Nobody'll notice." And, as Stella obeyed, she went

on. "Just let me talk to you for a little while, Mrs. Greeley; you'll be all right. There's something I've very much wanted to say to you ever since we knew that your husband was going to be the new factory manager. Do you mind if I go on?"

"I don't care what you do," Stella said moistly through the handkerchief which she now held applied to her nose. Sitting sidewise in her chair, so that her back was as much as possible toward the group of three at the other end of the room, she bent her head over the coffee cup upon her side of the little table. "I don't care what any of you say."

"And yet I might be able to say something that might make a little difference, Mrs. Greeley. At the reception after the inauguration banquet in honor of your husband, I naturally understood from your manner that you had a prejudice against me, and that was just what I'd been fearing. I'd been anxious to meet you and have a little talk with you before then in order to forestall that very prejudice; but the opportunity hadn't offered. You see, Mrs. Greeley, I knew beforehand that in all probability, you were going to form a very unfavorable opinion of me."

"Did you? I don't care."

Crystal leaned a little nearer her. "Mrs. Greeley,

I'm afraid you must let me make the matter clear to
you. Your husband's present position was formerly
held by Mr. Thomas, and before him by Mr. Peale.
When Mr. Peale had to resign, Mrs. Peale was very
bitter against me and afterward, when Mr. Thomas
in turn had to resign, Mrs. Thomas was just as furious with me as Mrs. Peale had been. Both women
did a lot of angry talking, and of course I knew that a
great many of the upper people in the N.K.U. were
familiar with their complaints against me. An institution like the N.K.U. has a social structure almost
exactly like that of general human society, itself:
when anything happens at the very top only the
people at the top, and nearest, know exactly the
truth of what has happened and, as accounts of it
are passed down from mouth to mouth, the story
is the more garbled the lower it goes, and, at the
same time, all the more eagerly do the lower circles
of people relish and enlarge the garblings. Mrs. Peale
and then Mrs. Thomas blamed me for their husbands'
being dropped; and that was because they thought
I had influenced Mr. Cooper. They knew of my
intimacy here—an intimacy that began in my girl-
hood, Mrs. Greeley, and before I went into the
N.K.U.—and they knew, too, that Mr. Cooper had

gradually come to depend upon me more and more."
She laughed deprecatingly. "I suppose I'm a sort of
watchdog for him, Mrs. Greeley. I'm there eight
hours a day to his two or three, and I have something
of his own passion for the efficiency of the place, and
he knows it. Mrs. Peale and Mrs. Thomas thought I
set him against their husbands, and Mr. Thomas
and Mr. Peale thought the same thing their wives
did; they naturally did not care to face the actual
fact that they weren't large enough men for the job—
that the true cause of their going was their own
failure. We're all like that more or less, of course; it's
natural for us to let ourselves down as easily as we
can, and I've never felt any rancor against the
Thomases and Peales for letting themselves down at
my expense. I didn't set Mr. Cooper against either
of those men, though, Mrs. Greeley; it was their
own mistakes that determined him. But it is true
that he consulted me and that together we very
reluctantly had to face the fact of those mistakes.
What's more he consulted me about the appointment
of your husband, and I was able to point out to him
that Mr. Greeley would never make such mistakes."
She laughed again, placatively. "I may be Mr.
Cooper's watchdog but I'm not there to bite your

husband; I'm not a spy upon him, Mrs. Greeley; I'm an enthusiast for him."

"I don't care what you are."

Crystal ventured to touch with light fingers, and but for an instant, her companion's cold hand now resting upon the little table and clutching the wet handkerchief. "Mrs. Greeley, I'm afraid I must try to make you care! I knew that in some form or other the story of Mrs. Thomas's and Mrs. Peale's bitterness would be likely to reach you, and that it would represent me as an intriguing, dangerous and power-seeking woman whose principal business was to be an enemy to the factory manager and to set the president of the N.K.U. against him. When you snubbed me at the reception, of course I saw that this misrepresentation had indeed reached you and that already you were prepared to treat me as your husband's potential enemy; and yet, if you had known it, I'd been doing quite a little that very day in the hope of showing you how much I wanted to be his friend and yours, Mrs. Greeley."

Stella's face had been lowered and averted; but at this, she turned her head and, from eyes still wetly glistening, looked sheerest incredulity. "What are you trying to put over on me now?"

Crystal shook her head ruefully. "Mr. Cooper wanted to have only men at the Speakers' Table at the banquet. I convinced him that he should have you there, and at his right. It was a compliment Mr. Greeley would like, I thought, and I believed it might please you. Also, I showed Mr. Cooper it was in line with his policy of being interested in the domestic life of his people—an honor to you might encourage other wives to feel that their services to their husbands had some recognition. In fact, I thought a great deal about you, Mrs. Greeley, but I'm afraid it seems now that I almost have to prove it." She laughed a little sadly. "The orchids you wore that night pleased you, didn't they?"

"What?"

"Yes," Crystal said, "I picked them out pretty carefully, and I'm afraid I wanted a little credit with you for doing it. I meant to ask you if you liked them, and so hint that my hand was in it; but you didn't give me much chance!"

Slowly the incredulity that was in Stella's eyes lost its sharpness and her look became completely blank; then she uttered a little gasp.

"Oh golly!"

Crystal went on: "Mrs. Greeley, it's of the utmost

importance that you should be an aid to your husband in his career. In him Mr. Cooper has found the right man for the right place, at last—a man who will increase the prosperity of the institution—and you know how many people depend upon its prosperity. I can be of great service in my way to Mr. Greeley, and I will, no matter what you do; but that will be a great deal easier, of course, if I have not his wife's enmity but her good will. In your new position you may necessarily have to lose some old friends, and of course that's too bad." She paused a moment, looking at Stella thoughtfully, even gravely. "The old intimacies of people who go up in the world aren't always best for them or for their early intimates, either; and our institution is compelled to make a great many changes in the lives of its people. I hope you won't regret the changes it makes in yours." She paused again, then leaned toward Stella with a friendly and charming smile. "Mrs. Greeley, as you inevitably must make some new friends, mayn't I hope to be one of them?"

Stella looked at her distractedly; then, as a noise was heard approaching the open doorway nearby, and the dry and crackling laugh of Leahart sounded there, denoting the advent of the gentlemen from the dining room, she almost unconsciously seized the hand of Crystal Nelson in a convulsive clasp.

"Say, I feel rotten!" she gasped. "Can't you get me out of here?"

Crystal retained Stella's hand tightly for a moment. "You're all right," she whispered. "You needn't do a thing but sit here quietly with me for a little while; nobody'll come near us. Mrs. Leahart's going to play; she's already at the piano. As soon as that's over, you can just get your husband and go and tell Mrs. Cooper good-night. You can manage it, can't you?"

"Oh golly! I guess so."

XV

WELL, anyway, we lived through it!" The good William mopped his cheerful face with his handkerchief when the oaken door of the stone house had closed behind him and Stella. "I thought once or twice I wasn't going to, myself, especially when that old yaller geezer of a Leahart got me cornered with one of his funny questions!" he said, as they crossed the terrace. "But, after all, people are just people, and a body can kind of talk along with this sort as well as any other, once you get over being scared of 'em. I guess on the whole I had a pretty good time after all; didn't you, Stella? You certainly put it all over everybody there for looks, anyhow. I guess we didn't come out so much at the little end of the horn after all, don't you think so, Stella?"

She said nothing, and they descended to the gravel path that led to the street where they had left their sedan. "Don't you think so, Stella?" he repeated, as they walked along the path together. "When that music talk started, with all that stuff about Schnickle-fritz and everybody that nobody ever heard of before, I certainly thought we were gone; but after a while when we kind of got used to it, I guess we made a pretty good stab at a showing. Glory! I'm certainly going to buy some books and read up before I get caught in a jam like that again. I expect we've got to start out and get ourselves all polished and cultivated up, Stella, now we're getting to go with the high and mighty!" He laughed a little excitedly. "We'll probably be inviting the Big Boss and his wife and a crowd like that to dinner, ourselves, before long, Stella, when we get into the new house. Woosh! I'm going to read up till I can talk like Schnicklefritz, himself, by that time! Hello!" he said, as they reached the end of the path. "What's this?"

Their sedan stood just in advance of a street lamp; the door was thrown open, and a woman's slight figure leaped out and came running toward them, silhouetted against the light. They heard her panting and gasping Stella's name before she reached them; it was Aurelia.

"Aurelia Hedge!" William exclaimed. "Where'd you come from? What's the matter?"

But Aurelia seized Stella by the shoulders. "You fixed it? For heaven's sake, Stella, tell me you fixed it!"

"Fixed what?" William asked, greatly astonished; and then, as the long and bent figure of Henry Hedge detached itself from the sedan, "What on earth are you two up to?"

"She wouldn't wait." Mr. Hedge explained drearily, coming toward them. "After I told her my news she made me walk all the way up here with her and get in your car and sit till you came out. She wouldn't listen to——"

"You be quiet!" his wife cried, and, retaining her hold upon Stella's shoulders, shook her. "Stella, for heaven's sake, aren't you going to tell me you got it fixed up for us?"

Her voice had become shrill, and Stella broke out at her angrily: "You let me alone! Take your hands off me and quit yelling like that! You want people to come out of that house and hear you making this disturbance?"

"Then why, in the name of heaven, can't you tell me if you've done what you said you would or not? What do you mean standing there and letting me——"

But here her voice had become so loud that both husbands intervened. Henry put his arm about her to draw her away, while William implored in an undertone: "Get back in the car. My glory! If you're going to have hysterics let's get away from here!"

They bundled her into the sedan with Stella beside her; William hurriedly mounted to the driver's seat and began to operate the controls; Mr. Hedge followed him, and they drove rapidly away.

"What are you holding out on me this way for?" Aurelia went on, with unabated vehemence. "What's the matter you can't answer when I——"

"Just hold your horses, Aurelia, can't you?" her husband interrupted, over his shoulder. "I told you it wouldn't do any good to come up here; we can't talk a thing like this over in a bumpy sedan. We'll be home in five minutes, so for mercy's sakes can't you wait?"

"Guess it looks like I got to," Aurelia assented bitterly. "If she can't answer a simple——"

"Well, you see she can't," Henry said, "so just wait, will you?"

Aurelia's rapid breathing was audible within the car; but she made no reply, and did not speak again until the Warwicke Armes had been reached and the four stood at the door of the Greeleys' apartment. There she addressed her husband sharply. "What'd you get off the elevator here for? You take Bill and go on up to our room, because I and Stella——"

"No," Henry said gloomily. "It's too late in the day for any female pow-wows. I'm going to be in on it, and I want Bill in on it, too. We four are going to talk this thing over together, Aurelia."

She looked at him defiantly, but his air was stubborn and determined; she gave way, and the two serious husbands followed their wives into the room. Stella went to the maroon velvet sofa and sat there, leaning back, staring pallidly upward at nothing. She seemed completely unaware of Aurelia who came at her angrily even before William had closed the door.

"Now look here, Stella Greeley, how long before you're going to tell me——"

"Wait a minute! Wait a minute!" William interrupted, coming from the door. "Give a man a chance to find out a little of what's been going on, can't you? You sit down, Aurelia, and keep quiet a minute or so. Henry, what's it all about?"

Mr. Hedge made no oral reply; but in silence drew from his pocket a folded sheet of paper and handed it to William. Then, producing one of his bad cigars, he lighted it and seated himself droopingly, yet had spirit enough left to elevate his feet upon the gilt radiator. William read the letter aloud, slowly.

"DEAR SIR:—

"I am instructed to write you as follows:

"In accordance with the new policy of the N.K.U. an examination of the record of Promotion Marks is now made every ten days and the present examination, concluded only last evening, entails certain changes in the personnel of your department. No complaint against your service there has been received and this notification does not mean that your work has been found specially unsatisfactory. Therefore you should not consider the change we are making as a demotion for yourself and you will be continued in your new position at your present salary. Mr. C. W. Crosse, until now manager of our chain-hardware store at Bennettsville, this State, is shown by the Promotion Mark system to be entitled to a position in one of the headquarters departments, and thus the managership he has so well filled is left vacant. You are hereby notified to proceed to Bennettsville by the fifteenth of this present month, as

Mr. Crosse will be leaving upon the sixteenth, and you will assume at once the duties entailed by the managership of the Bennettsville chain store. Your appointment to this position seems peculiarly appropriate because of your former residence in Bennettsville and your acquaintance with the citizens of that place. We trust that the removal of your household goods will not entail great inconvenience through shortness of the time allowed for such removal, as it is imperative that you report at your post in Bennettsville on the morning of the fifteenth. We believe that in this new service you will be effective and useful, and that under your guidance our enterprise there will be conducted as successfully as heretofore under Mr. Crosse.

"We remain yours truly

"J. C. PENDLETON, *Secretary P. M. Records*."

"There!" Aurelia cried. "I guess maybe you'll talk some now, Stella! Are you going to keep on sitting there in a trance or are you going to answer my——"

But once more her husband stopped her. "Wait just a minute, can't you?" He stretched forth a thin hand and took the letter from William. "One of the messengers handed it to me just before I left the

office yesterday afternoon. I didn't want to spoil the
party last night for Aurelia by telling her about it
then, and anyway, I wanted to wait for a chance
when we could all four be together to talk it over.
Stella and Aurelia have been pretty good friends,
and I kind of wanted Stella with her when she heard
it. I was kind of cowardly about it, I guess. I had my
mouth open to tell you, Bill, a dozen times, when we
were out in the sedan this afternoon, but you looked
kind of down yourself, and I just waited. Then to-
night, after you and Stella had gone out to this dinner,
Aurelia, poor thing, got to talking big about all this
and that we were going to do—how I was going to
get a raise and we were going to rent a fine, big
house, and all thus and so; I just couldn't stand to let
her go on. She was dancing around the room, and she
said a little bird had told her all about what big good
luck was coming to us, and everything; it seemed to
me I couldn't let her believe such nonsense any
longer, so I showed her the letter. Well, at first she
laughed at it and pooh-poohed; she said she didn't
care anything about Cooper's New Policy and the
Promotion Mark system; all that stuff cut no ice
with her; she had everything fixed for us. But of
course she couldn't keep that up long after such a

letter as this, and pretty soon she got so rattled that nothing would do but for us to go up there to Cooper's and wait till you came out. I knew it wouldn't do any good." He shook his head sadly. "I never dreamed but I was doing my work as well as any man in our department, but I guess somebody don't think so. Anyhow, it's back to Bennettsville for ours, and I guess the best thing Stella can do is help Aurelia make her mind up to it."

"Is it?" Aurelia said shrilly. "Is that the best thing Stella can do? She better not try it, because you can bet your last dollar we're not going back to Bennettsville! Not much! Don't think you'll ever get me back in that old cross-roads mudhole; don't think it for a minute! Did you hear what that crazy letter said?" She laughed contemptuously. "It says by the fifteenth! That's Tuesday—Tuesday of this week, day after to-morrow! I see myself in Bennettsville day after to-morrow, or any other time!" She jumped up from the chair where she had seated herself at William's command, went to Stella and stood before her, trembling and furious. "Look here, Stella Greeley——"

Stella did not move. "Can't you let me alone?" she said.

"Let you alone? Are you crazy? You needn't think I don't know why you don't dare to talk? You didn't do what you promised me you would, and you're ashamed to tell me you didn't. You went in that house and you got so busy showing off and putting on airs and being all fol-lol and high society, you went back on me. Yes, you did! You'd never have amounted to anything if it hadn't been for me; you wouldn't even have had a decent dress to wear to-night! But the minute you get a chance to show off at a high society dinner you think somebody's going to look down on you if you let 'em see that Henry and I are intimate friends of yours, and so you decide to go back on your word and not even mention us. Do you know what you begin to look like to me? You begin to look like the kind that the minute they get up the ladder, themselves, turn around and kick their old friends in the face!"

"She isn't, either," William said stoutly, "Stella isn't anything of the sort; she wouldn't——"

"Wouldn't she?" Aurelia cried. "That's just what she's done. Why look at her! She can't say a word. If she'd done the right thing by Henry and me wouldn't it 'a' been the first thing she told us the minute she saw us waiting outside Cooper's house?

She wouldn't sit here now and let me accuse her if she had anything to say for herself, would she?"

"She would if she didn't know what you were accusing her of, as I certainly don't."

"You think she doesn't know?" Aurelia laughed shrewishly. "I'll tell you something she's going to know mighty soon, and that is she can't treat me like this and get away with it! She made a promise to me and she's going to keep it; she's going to keep it to-night, too; it's not too late. If any of you think the whole N.K.U. can get me back in Bennettsville I'll show you you're mistaken!" And with that, she ran to the little table that served for a telephone stand. "I'll show you!"

But her husband intercepted her; he jumped up and took the instrument from her hands as she lifted it. "What on earth are you doing, Aurelia?"

"You keep away from me. Let me have that 'phone. I know what I'm doing. Let me have it, I say!"

"What for?"

"I'll show Stella Greeley what for. I'm going to call Cooper up, and she's going to talk to him and do what she promised. You let me have that 'phone. Take your hands off of it, I say!" Half screaming, she tried to wrench her husband's fingers from the instrument, and fought him for possession of it. "You let go, Henry Hedge; I tell you I know what I'm doing! I'm going to call Cooper up, and Stella's going to——"

"Take the 'phone," Henry said desperately to William; and then, as the latter obeyed, contrived to twist the frantic woman away and force her down into a chair. "She'll have you in Bennettsville, too, if we're not careful." Then he spoke to the writhing and panting Aurelia. "What you trying to do? Ruin everybody?"

William stood aghast. "What was she going to call Cooper for?"

"She wasn't," Mr. Hedge said, with a wry smile. "That's just a bluff because she's sore at Stella. She let out a good deal while we were waiting in your car. Seems they planned Stella was going to tackle Cooper at the dinner and get him to give me a raise! Of course as soon as you came out, we saw that Stella'd had too much sense to make such a fool of herself and—at least I hope it was that way." He turned gloomily to Stella. "You didn't do anything like that, did you, Stella, and get turned down? You didn't say anything to him, did you?"

"No," Stella said, not moving. "I didn't."

Aurelia had begun to weep. "You're going to," she said. "Don't think for a minute I'll stand for your turning yellow on me! You had the whole thing in your hands and you——"

"How did she?" William interrupted sharply. "What did Stella have in her hands?"

"Cooper," Aurelia sobbed. "She knows he'd have done it if she'd asked him, and she's got to do it yet!"

"Stella!" William said incredulously. "Why, Aurelia, if anybody could ask Cooper a thing like that I could, and of course I would, but Henry knows, himself, as well as I do, I might just as well ask him to burn up the whole N.K.U. works, for all the good it would do. Everybody in the N.K.U. knows the danger of approaching him on a point like that; once he's issued an edict, it's law, and if he thought Henry'd asked me to intercede for him—which is what he would think—Henry mightn't even get Bennettsville." He turned to his wife. "Stella, you didn't have it in mind to do anything as foolish as that, did you?"

Stella shook her head slowly. "Not after I set foot in that house. I guess this was what she meant."

"What who meant?"

"That woman," Stella said huskily. "She told me that I was going to be separated from friends of mine; she said the N.K.U. was making changes and I'd have to get new friends. She knew what she was talking about because——" Stella's voice became so low and indistinct that as she finished expressing this thought she was audible to no one but herself: "Because she'd done it herself, I guess."

Aurelia stared at her. "Who? What woman are you talking about?"

"Crystal Nelson."

"What!" And Aurelia's mouth dropped open. "Crystal Nelson! Do you mean she was at——"

"Why, yes," William informed her, "she was there to-night and it looked to me as if she's there half the time anyway; she's certainly Mrs. Cooper's most intimate friend, and I guess she's pretty much the same thing with him, too. She and Mrs. Cooper go on trips, and you could tell by the way they were arguing together about music that they think the world and all of each other. Why, Miss Nelson——"

"Crystal Nelson!" Aurelia cried again, and her face, her voice and her stricken attitude expressed a gathering horror. "*She* told you——"

"Yes," Stella said, "this was what she meant, and

I expect she thought I already knew about it and wanted to make me understand it as a—as a——"
Her voice, already husky, broke pathetically. Then she concluded: "She wanted me to understand it as a—as a sort of warning or—or more like a punishment, maybe."

"Punishment?" William repeated. "What for?"

"Well, maybe," she answered, and she looked up at him drearily. "Maybe because I was overdressed, or something."

"Why, what——"

But Aurelia interrupted him; she turned fiercely upon her husband. "You look here! Right now you got to act like a man for once in your life. We're out of the N.K.U. for good; do you understand? To-morrow you're going to tell the N.K.U. to go to hell, and you're going out and get a job right here in this city. You're going to every other big firm there is, and you're going to——"

Mr. Hedge uttered a loud and prolonged laugh in despair of her intelligence. Then he slumped down into his chair by the radiator. "Fat chance!" he said.

Aurelia knew her doom and she could not accept it without agony. She jumped up and struck her husband's drooping shoulders two violent blows with

clenched fists. "What am I tied to you for?" she
asked him hoarsely. "Why couldn't I have got a man
instead of an old rag of a thing like you that lets
everybody ride over him and can't even make a
squeak for himself. A pretty life you've made for me!
I put a little spirit and ambition into you and got
you out of Bennettsville and up here to the city just
long enough to make it a black hell for me to have
to go back there; and now that's what we've got to
do. You let Bill Greeley walk right up over your
shoulders and tramp you down under, and you take
me with you into the mud, and you haven't got man-
hood enough to lift one finger to save me. Half the
women in the N.K.U. will be crowing over me
to-morrow, and yet you sit there with your feet up
and your cigar sticking out of your mouth! What do
you care! You got to slink back to Bennettsville
and drag me with you——" But despair caught at her
throat, and the shrill voice broke into a passion of
sobbing. "Oh, my Lord, that's where I end up! A
hardware dealer's wife in a jay town! Oh, my Lord!
that's where I end up!"

The thin and melancholy head of Henry Hedge
nodded forlornly; his chin sank a little deeper into
the collar that was too large for his neck, and the ash

of his cigar dropped upon his waistcoat, thence drifted downward to the hardwood floor as he slowly got upon his feet. Then he put his arm about the convulsing form of his wife, and spoke to her in a voice a little tremulous. "It's hard luck, Aurelia. I—I didn't know but I was doing about as well as anyone in my department; I didn't have any idea I wasn't giving good satisfaction or—or was slipping, or anything. But it seems they think I was, and when they think so that's all there is to it—a man's up against it. It's hard luck but we got to go, Aurelia." Thus speaking, he urged her gently toward the door, and she submitted to this pressure. "There isn't anything for it; all we can do is to begin getting our things packed up to-night because we'll have to leave sometime to-morrow afternoon. We'll see you folks to-morrow, so we won't say good-bye now. Aurelia, could you manage to hush up a little till we get through the hall and up the elevator? You can let out all you want again soon as we get up to our own room." Then, at the door, as Aurelia struggled for the control he besought of her, he looked back apologetically over his shoulder. "Of course I must have been slipping or something, or they wouldn't have done it; so I guess she's right—I've brought this down on her. And all so sudden and everything, it's going to be a little hard for her to get used to it. You mustn't blame her for being upset; she didn't really mean anything she said to Stella, Bill, or all this and that about your climbing up on my shoulders and pushing me down. It was just easing off her disappointment because she thought she and Stella had everything all fixed up;—of course it was foolish but they meant for the best."

With that, he gave utterance to a troubled and wistful sound of laughter, bade his friends good-night, led his shaking wife out of the room and closed the door.

XVI

WHEN William and his wife were thus left alone together she still sat upon the sofa, looking blankly forward at nothing; but he began to pace the floor in a profound and frowning cogitation. For a time, his footsteps made the only sounds audible within the room; then the rumbling of the ascending elevator, the clicking of its door in the corridor, and a cheerful babbling of voices calling good-nights gave evidence that a party of denizens had returned to the Warwicke Armes, probably after a "second show" at the movies and subsequent libations at a soda fountain. The noise, nocturnally customary, subsided without William's having been consciously aware of it; yet some part of him may have received mechanically a warning of the lateness of the hour, for his pacing back and forth stopped abruptly; he sat down in a chair near his wife and, still frowning heavily, faced her.

"There's something I've got to get at, Stella," he said slowly. "Last night after what Mrs. Gliesinger told me I asked you if you'd been talking, and then you got so upset about a dress for this dinner to-night and all, I couldn't go on with it. Well, I've been thinking. The way Mrs. Gliesinger had it I was supposed to be jealous—Lord knows what about!—but everybody understands how gossip gets twisted once it begins going around, and it looks to me as if Mrs. Gliesinger had founded what she said on a twisted version of your jealousy about Miss Crystal Nelson and me. Anyhow, it's clear that stories about us have been going around and I can't get it out of my head that it's got something to do with the way Aurelia's been acting to-night. Of course she was just wild with disappointment; it's a terrible thing for a bright, ambitious woman like Aurelia to have to realize that she's going down in the world, not up, and I feel almost as sorry for her as I do for poor old Henry; but there was something queer about the way she took it. At first she was fighting mad—she just wasn't going to have it—and then, the minute you mentioned Miss Nelson's name, she laid right down. Just as soon as she heard about Crystal Nelson's being Mr. and Mrs. Cooper's closest friend, Aurelia gave up; she was all through. Why, she just collapsed! Now that strikes me as pretty funny,

Stella; I can't help thinking it has some connection. How does it strike you?"

Stella did not look at him; and her eyes, under drooping lashes, wandered to a corner of the floor. "I don't know," she murmured. "I wasn't thinking much about it."

"Well, I am," he said with emphasis. "I'm thinking a whole lot about it. And there's something else: Aurelia said you had the 'whole thing' in your hands, and when I asked her what she meant you had in your hands she said 'Cooper'! What did she mean by that?"

But Stella's lowered glance remained upon the corner of the floor. "How do I know? I don't know what Aurelia meant by—by anything."

"Are you sure you don't?" He leaned forward, scrutinizing her gravely. "You and Aurelia have always been thick but lately you've been thicker than ever; you've had pow-wows alone together all day most of the time. It isn't easy for me to believe that you didn't understand everything she said. I want to know why she collapsed at the name of Crystal Nelson and why she said you had Cooper where he'd do anything you asked him."

"I don't know," Stella returned with a hint of

doggedness in her low voice; and she still looked away from him. "I don't know what Aurelia meant."

"You know what it sounded as if she meant. You know that much, don't you?"

"What?"

"It sounded to me as if you and Aurelia had been flying pretty high in these pow-wows you've been holding all day and half the night," he said, and his voice was stern. "One of the things you told me lately that I haven't forgotten was that you put me where I am. At the time you said it I thought you meant your influence on me but it begins to look as if you meant your influence on Cooper. Your influence on Cooper!" He repeated the words ruefully and contemptuously. "If he knew you thought you had any, it might come pretty near costing me my job, even though he knows the N.K.U. needs me. Is that what you want to have happen?"

"No."

"Do you think you've got any influence on Cooper?"

"No."

"Well, what Aurelia said sounded as if she thought you've got a good deal, didn't it? Answer me!"

Upon this, she tried to look at him but failed; her eyelids fluttered and her glance went back to the corner. "I can't help how it sounded. I suppose it sounded as if prob'ly she thought Mr. Cooper kind of liked me and so maybe it wouldn't do any harm for me to say a word to him about Henry—if I got the chance."

"So? What made her think that?"

"What did?" Stella's eyelids fluttered again; there was a troubled movement of her throat as if she swallowed and she spoke with difficulty. "Well, I guess it was what Mr. Cooper said about me that night at the—at the banquet."

"Is that all?"

"Well, she might—she might have exaggerated it some. I guess I—I did, myself, maybe—until I walked into that house to-night!"

William shook his head. "There's something behind it. What made Aurelia collapse when she heard Crystal Nelson was there?"

Stella was able to meet his eyes at last. "I don't know," she said. "I tell you I honestly don't know— not unless Aurelia'd said something to somebody about my being jealous and thought maybe Miss Nelson might have heard she'd said it."

"Weren't you and Miss Nelson sitting together most of this evening after you left the table?"

"Yes, we were."

"Well, she looked to me as if she was being pretty friendly and polite, wasn't she?"

"Yes, she was."

"Then how do you explain it?" he insisted.

"I don't know. I guess Miss Nelson'd be that way, no matter what."

He seemed to acquiesce in this; then brooded gloomily for a moment. "How'd she happen to tell you that Henry was going to lose his job here?"

"She didn't say it in so many words but something she said sounded afterwards like she'd meant that."

"Yes—maybe she did. I guess there's mighty little happens in the N.K.U. that she doesn't know beforehand, and I expect it's a pretty good thing for us that she's always shown heself friendly and helpful to me. But there's something behind all this I don't get at; I'm pretty sure you know more than you're telling me and I mean to have it out of you, Stella. Right here, to begin with, though, I've got a question to ask you that I think it's about time you answered!"

"Have you?"

"Yes, I have!" Unsatisfied upon the other points he had been pressing, he spoke with indignation upon this one; he rose and stood looking down at her angrily. "I want to ask you: when you met Miss Nelson to-night weren't you ashamed of the way you'd been talking to me about her—yes, and talking about her and me to God knows who! Yes, and letting Aurelia talk for you, too! There's one thing I would like to know from you right now: I want you to look me in the eye and tell me if you weren't ashamed to-night!"

"Ashamed?" Stella quavered, and her eyes at this sharp bidding rose flickeringly to meet his for a moment. Then she shivered; her lovely figure trembled and she slid over upon the sofa, face downward, her arms as if protectingly about her head upon the maroon velvet cushion. She lay there, silent.

William looked down at that stricken and helpless form from which the strips of rhinestones and the sunburst of false diamonds seemed to glitter up at him coldly, yet with a reproachful pathos.

"I guess you better get to bed," he said. "I mean to go to the bottom of this business, Stella; but right now I expect you better try to get some sleep."

HE GOT little sleep himself until near daylight, and then he slumbered so heavily that when he woke the sun was high and it was time for him to be at his office. Stella was not in the room; she had risen without disturbing him and gone out—to Aurelia, he grimly supposed. She had left the electric percolator ready for his use, however, and sliced bread in the electric toaster; he made a hasty breakfast and would have sallied forth upon the instant of its conclusion; but at the door he paused and turned to the telephone. He called the number of the Hedges' apartment and was surprised when the voice of Henry responded.

William laughed dryly. "You there, Henry? They haven't sent you out yet?"

"Who haven't sent me out?"

"Stella and Aurelia."

"Stella isn't here," Mr. Hedge returned. "She sent Aurelia's rhinestones up in a package by the elevator man; but we haven't seen her. We packed till two

o'clock last night and got up at six and started again."
He laughed feebly. "No great trouble about that; we
haven't got much to pack. The sedan's in the shop
and it won't be out till Wednesday or Thursday; but
the janitor's going to put the phonograph and the
radio in it and hire somebody to drive it down to
Bennettsville for us by the end of the week."

"Couldn't I attend to that for you, Henry?"

"No; it's all looked out for."

"Well, isn't there something else I can do for you,
Henry?"

"Not a thing, Bill."

William insisted. "I wish you'd let me. I'd do anything I know how, Henry."

"I know you would, Bill."

"Then look here, Henry: if you think it'd be the
least good on earth for me to go to Cooper——"

The voice of Mr. Hedge occupied in lugubrious
laughter cut short the offer. "Don't do that unless
you want to fix me up with no job at all. Thank you
just the same."

"What time are you and Aurelia going to leave?"

"Four forty-five."

"I'll be there," William promised. "I've got to be
off to the works now, Henry, and I'm tied up with a

business luncheon; but I'll be at the train. Stella and I'll both be there to tell you good-bye; but of course Stella'll be up to see you before that; she and Aurelia'll probably want to spend most of this last day together."

In this supposition, however, he found himself mistaken: Stella did not come to the station to bid her unfortunate old friends farewell, nor had Aurelia seen her at all since the preceding night. Aurelia did not voluntarily mention this but gave the information in reply to a question; her tone was something more than preoccupied and even something more than indifferent, he thought; in fact it seemed to him that she was relieved when the final moment of parting came without Stella's having appeared. He watched the train move out of the station bearing with it the patient, long face of Henry Hedge dustily framed at the window of a day coach, and William sighed deeply as that forlorn and never unkindly visage thus passed permanently from his view.

"The poor old cuss," he murmured. "I wish I knew——" His mind had returned again to his perplexities; and to these there was added a slight new puzzlement: Why hadn't Stella come?

Debating within himself upon this and more serious

matters, he drove away from the station in the new, light automobile he had bought for his own use, and, leaving the crowded highways of business behind him, sped northward toward the new boulevards and the Warwicke Armes. Stella was there by this time, he supposed as he passed that edifice; but he decided that he did not wish to see her just then; he had intended to stop and go up to their apartment and to renew the process begun last night of wringing the truth from her—for the truth he would have, one way or another!—but he did not stop. For some reason not quite known to him the thought of the little apartment, and particularly of the maroon colored sofa, made him feel sickish; and although he swerved to turn in toward the portals of the Warwicke Armes he set his car upon a straight course again and continued to move northward. He would go out to the new house, he thought; it had been vacated by its former tenants a week earlier; it stood empty now and he had a key to the front door in his pocket.

But no easement of mind came to him when he got out of the little automobile and stood facing the house. It was brick covered with whitewash and agreeable enough in mass and outline—"English Cottage" in type, the agent had told him. There were some fine trees behind it and, in front, shrubberies, a pleasant, small lawn and a green hedge. William had expected to be happy here; but he had no such expectation now, and as he went frowningly up the cement path the air of gayety that had once seemed to be about the little place was vanished. "What's the use!" he said aloud.

He inserted his key in the lock but did not turn it, for the handle yielded under the pressure of his fingers and the door opened. "Somebody here?" he called inquiringly as he passed within.

There was no response; he went through the empty rooms of the lower floor and then, ascending the stairs, began to search the second story. The door of the largest room at the front of the house—the room to be his bedchamber and Stella's—was closed, and he went to it last. When he opened the door he saw a woman sitting upon a pine box near the window and apparently engaged in looking out at the street beyond the lawn. It was Stella.

"What are you doing here?" he asked, after a moment.

"Nothing. I've been here all day."

"Did you walk up here this morning before I got

up?" She nodded; and he inquired, "Where'd you go for lunch?"

"I didn't want any. The telephone's working and I got that decorator out here again this afternoon. He just left a while ago; but I was glad when he was gone. He wants us to put up plum colored drapes downstairs and he wants us to have maroon rugs and a maroon colored sofa—velvet."

"No, for pity's sake!" William broke out vehemently. "Don't let's have any——"

"I told him I wouldn't," Stella said. "I told him I wouldn't have any maroon in the whole house. He was bound to; but I told him I wouldn't have it."

"You told him right!" William rejoined grimly; then he came into the room and stood near her. "Stella, why didn't you come to the train to tell Henry and Aurelia good-bye?"

"To tell them good-bye?"

"That's what I said! Why didn't you?" Stella had not turned toward him and she continued to look out of the window. "Why didn't you?" he repeated impatiently.

"I guess I didn't care much about it."

"You didn't? When it was your last chance to see Aurelia for probably——"

"I don't care," she said pettishly. "I don't care anything about seeing Aurelia. I wouldn't care if I never saw her again."

He pondered upon this before he spoke. "You say that because you and she are angry with each other about something. I see."

"No," Stella returned, and she laughed bleakly. "I'm not a bit angry with her and she isn't with me."

"Then why——"

"I just don't care one way or the other. I don't care whether I ever do see her or whether I ever don't see her any more."

Here the tone in which she spoke, drearily indifferent, carried conviction; and the fact was made plain to him that without having quarrelled neither of these two friends, who had been such close companions and busy confidantes, cared to see the other again. More, it seemed to him that neither of them even cared what became of the other; so completely had some mysterious thing severed them. Two men who had shared such a companionship would not part with each other in this strange way; men broke comradeships, yes; but when they broke them abruptly like this there was feeling—anger or disgust or at least regret—there was never silent, utter indifference; they didn't each merely pass the other into oblivion. But here, William knew he confronted the hopelessly inexplicable; he was only a man standing outside of what was forever impenetrably feminine. William was practical and experience had taught him that the fact of his wife's being a woman permanently precluded him from comprehending many mental and emotional processes within her; this was one of them—a closed stone door she could not herself have opened to him. Irritated, he could only helplessly pass it by and go on to what was possible.

"Listen," he said. "After I'd seen them off a while ago I thought I'd go up home; I thought you'd be there. But when I got to the apartment I just couldn't make myself stop and go up; it pretty near turned my stomach to think of."

"Did it?" Stella murmured, and as she had doggedly looked at the corner of the floor last night, so she now continued to look out of the window and down at the street. Nothing was there visible to interest her, nor had she any heed of the passing automobiles conveying women home from matinées and downtown shops or relaxed men of business from their daily labors. Then an unfamiliar sound came clicking rhythmically from the boulevard;

iron horseshoes rang upon the asphalt and Milton
Cooper came into view riding a bay horse debonairly
homeward from the near-by park. The bleakness of
Stella's expression as she looked at him suffered no
more alteration than when she had just now vaguely
thought and spoken of Aurelia Hedge, for this fine
figure of a horseman trotting by had been subjected
to transformation by another of those strange inner
processes behind stone doors impenetrable to William.
Not a shred of romance hung still upon the garments
of the equestrian. Already he had become for her
almost what he had been before William's promotion,
a distant shape, impersonal except that it was re-
motely formidable; so quickly had receded the glittering heroine and hero and the whole brilliant ballet
spectacle that had danced in her fancy. It receded
still farther, fading to nothingness with the receding
of Aurelia Hedge—— Stella had a faint consciousness
of a pale Aurelia on the train growing ever paler and
more transparent with the increasing distance until
she had no outlines at all—and, with this dissolving
of Aurelia and the shimmering ballet, all that had
seemed an absorbing reality was become thin air. It
appeared incredible to Stella that what was in truth
such mere mist and phantasm should leave conse-

quences after its passing—yet here stood her husband waiting for her to speak, and she had nothing to tell him that was not ruinous.

The horseman passed beyond the scope of the window; the metallic pulsations of the hoof beats grew fainter, and then were gone without William's having been aware of them, for he had not taken his eyes from his wife's downcast profile. He had spared her last night; but all day the commiseration that postponed her ordeal had appeared to him more and more as a weakness; he would postpone it no longer.

"Stella——" he began harshly.

"Yes," she murmured, and through the tremulous half whisper in which she spoke there ran a faintly perceptible bitterness. "Yes, I guess you've got to!"

"Stella——"

She looked up at him, and he stopped speaking, for this upward look of hers startled him by its resemblance to one that he had seen, upon occasion, long ago;—he was a little shocked to find that the piteous eyes of his wife should remind him of the eyes of that old dog of his. He had often boasted to the other boys that it was the best dog in Bennettsville; but sometimes it got excited about chasing something, and ran away for a while; and when it humbly came home again, creeping into the yard, William brought forth the strap that held his schoolbooks together. Just before the first blow fell the little old dog would always look up at him entreatingly and yet submissively, understanding that there would be no mercy. "I couldn't help running away," the look seemed to say. "I just couldn't help it. You're going to half kill me, I know; but anyhow can't you believe that I just couldn't help it?"

William began again. "Stella, the first thing I want to know——" But his voice was unsteady as he gazed down into the eyes lifted so helplessly to his; he coughed loudly. He would talk about something else for a few moments, he decided, and then begin the severe questioning of her upon which he was determined. "I was just thinking," he said. "I was just thinking it might be a good thing if we could get moved up here right away."

Upon that, her upward gaze became one of incredulity. "What?"

"Do you suppose we could get in by the first of next week if we hurried?"

"I don't know," she said slowly. "Maybe we could. I've written a list of the furniture we'd need to start with."

"Where is it?"

"I left it downstairs on the dining-room mantel-piece. Shall I—shall I get it?"

He hesitated, frowning; then said, "I suppose you might as well."

But when she had left the room he was sorry that he had permitted this interruption; it was only some more weak shilly-shallying, he thought, and when she came back he would put an end to it. He would make her face him with the truth, the whole truth and nothing but the truth; and he framed in his mind the opening phrases of what he would say to her as soon as she appeared. "That list can wait, Stella, because we may never use it. What won't wait are some questions I didn't ask you last night and I warn you to answer them truthfully. I expect you'll probably try to lie to me but it won't be any use, Stella, so you might as well——"

Her footsteps, light but ascending slowly, were heard upon the stairs; he put his hands in his pockets, faced the door and stood waiting ominously.

"I found it," she said, as she reached the head of the stairway. "I thought I'd left it on the dining-room mantelpiece; but it wasn't there—it was on the window seat." She laughed apologetically. "I guess I'm getting forgetful or something." Then, with the sound of her apologetic laughter still audible as it dwindled to a murmur, she came timidly into the room. "I—I guess maybe I'm getting old or dumb or something. But anyway here it is." And she offered him the sheet of pencilled paper she had brought with her.

He meant not to take it; he meant to push her hand aside and say, "No more shilly-shallying! We're going to have it out between us right here and now, Stella!" But the hand that should have pushed hers aside remained in his pocket, and what he said severely was, "You read it to me. I have trouble enough reading your writing when you use a pen and ink and do it carefully. When you write in pencil nobody on earth can make anything of it."

"I guess that's so," she assented gently, and she began to read the list. After a moment she stopped and stood frowning at the paper.

"What's the matter?"

"Oh, dear," she laughed, "you're right; here's something I can't even read myself!"

This was his opportunity; he would begin the inquisition now—but again his powers failed him. All he did was to take the paper from her and decipher the scribbled words that had baffled her. "Towels," he said irritably. "It couldn't be trowels because even you wouldn't want two dozen trowels. Yes, here's the word 'dish' before it—dish towels. My goodness! Can't you read your own writing?" He returned the paper to her with an impatient gesture and, turning away from her abruptly, put his hands in his pockets and stood looking out of the window while she went on with the reading. Two or three of the items bothered her and she stumbled over them; but he did not interrupt or again offer to help her, and, as she continued, her voice took on a tone a little brisker and more confident.

The great Dutch King of England never did a better thing than when he destroyed, without reading it, the scroll bearing the names of those who had conspired against him. They had been traitors but would be truer to him thenceforth than if they knew he knew them for traitors; William of Orange let them live in safety and with spirits unbroken. By instinct sheerly, this other William did as fine a thing. He heard the lift in his wife's voice.

"Ah well," the good fellow said to himself. "I guess I can get along without knowing every last thing about everything."

THE END